"HE WOULD HAVE STUCK THAT OFFICER LIKE A PIG IF HE HAD SEEN HIM THEN. IT'S TRUE, TOO! SOME PEOPLE DON'T DESERVE MUCH MERCY."

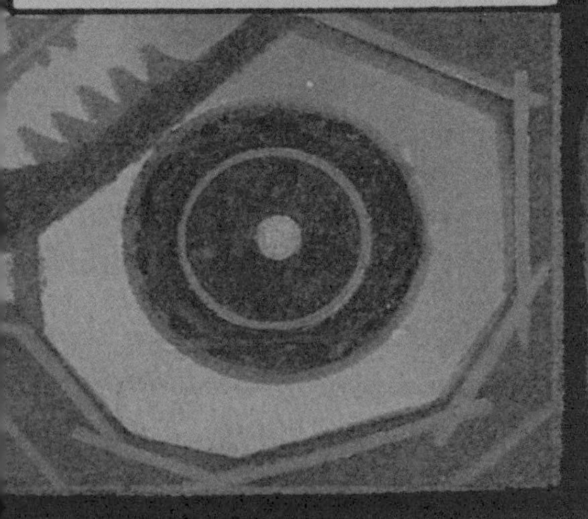

JOSEPH CONRAD

THE SECRET AGENT

adapted by

JOHN K. SNYDER III

writer, artist

PAUL FRICKE

letterer

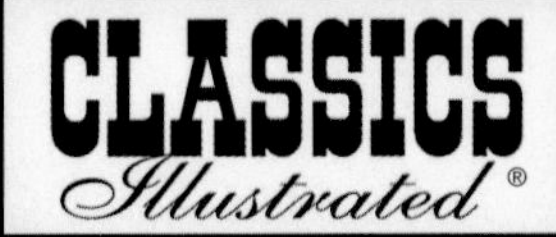

Featuring Stories by the World's Greatest Authors

PAPERCUTZ™

CLASSICS ILLUSTRATED GRAPHIC NOVELS AVAILABLE FROM PAPERCUTZ

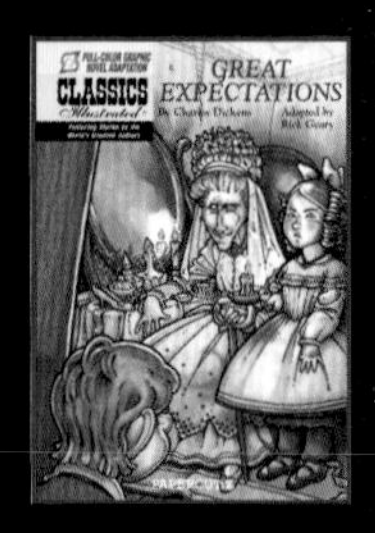

#1 "GREAT EXPECTATIONS"

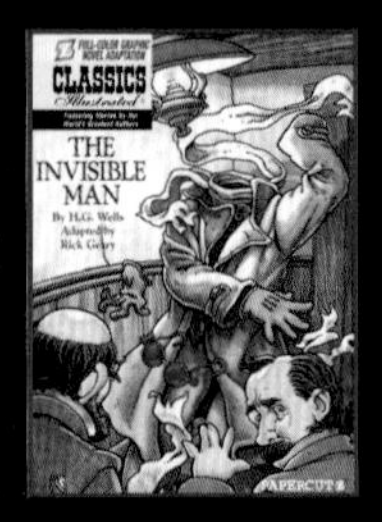

#2 "THE INVISIBLE MAN"

#3 "THROUGH THE LOOKING-GLASS"

#4 "THE RAVEN AND OTHER POEMS"

#5 "HAMLET"

#6 "THE SCARLET LETTER"

#7 "DR. JEKYLL & MR. HYDE"

#8 "THE COUNT OF MONTE CRISTO"

#9 "THE JUNGLE"

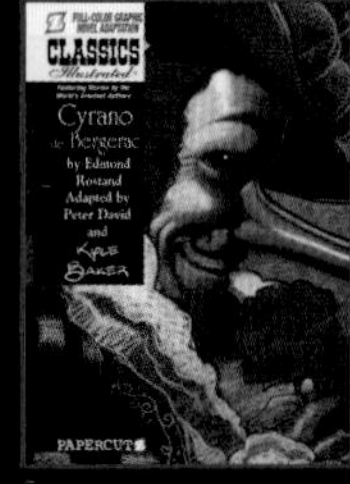

#10 "CYRANO DE BERGERAC"

#11 "THE DEVIL'S DICTIONARY AND OTHER WORKS"

#12 "THE ISLAND OF DOCTOR MOREAU"

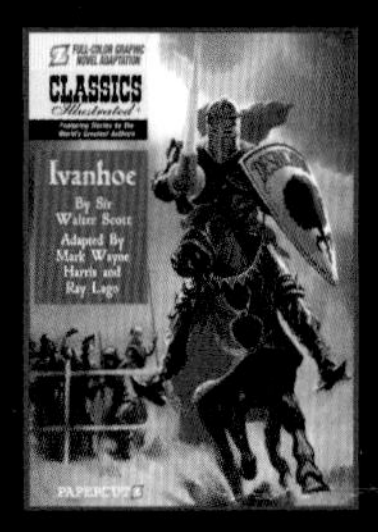

#13 "IVANHOE"

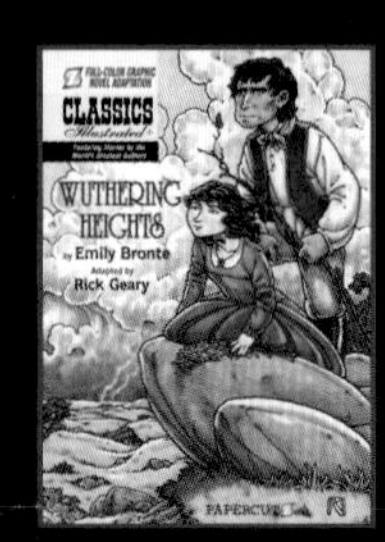

#14 "WUTHERING HEIGHTS"

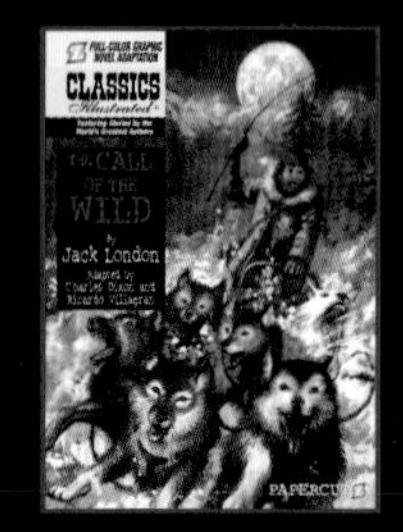

#15 "THE CALL OF THE WILD"

#16 "KIDNAPPED"

#17 "THE SECRET AGENT"

COMING SOON: #18 "AESOP'S FABLES"

CLASSICS ILLUSTRATED graphic novels are available only in hardcover for $9.95 each, except #8-18, $9.99 each. Available from booksellers everywhere.

Or order from us. Please add $4.00 for postage and handling for the first book, add $1.00 for each additional book. MC, Visa, Amex accepted or make check payable to NBM Publishing. Send to: Papercutz, 160 Broadway, Suite 700, East Wing, New York, NY 10038.

THE SECRET AGENT

Joseph Conrad

Adapted by

John K. Snyder III

A dark, suspenseful vision of terrorism, **The Secret Agent** is the most personal of Joseph Conrad's haunting works. The story of Verloc – his secret life as a double agent, his alliance with cold-blooded anarchists, and his part in a barbarous act – provides a compelling look at the corruption of beliefs. John K. Snyder's eerie paintings summon up the dark, chilling underworld of Conrad's spellbinding tale, the forerunner of the modern espionage thriller.

The Secret Agent
By Joseph Conrad
Adapted by John K. Snyder III
Paul Fricke -- letterer
Wade Roberts -- Original Editorial Director
Mike McCormick -- Original Art Director
Big Bird Zatryb -- Production
Classics Illustrated Historians -- John Haufe and William B. Jones Jr.
Beth Scorzato -- Production Coordinator
Michael Petranek -- Editor
Jim Salicrup
Editor-in-Chief

ISBN: 978-1-59707-416-2

Printed in China
March 2013 by New Era Printing LTD
Unit C, 8/F, Worldwide Centre
123 Tung Chau St, Kowloon, Hong Kong

Distributed by Macmillan.

First Papercutz Printing

Mr. Verloc, going out in the morning, left his shop nominally in charge of his brother-in-law. It could be done, because there was very little business at any time, and practically none at all before the evening. Mr. Verloc cared but little about his ostensible business.

RING
RING
The door of the shop was the only means of entrance to the house in which Mr. Verloc carried on his business of shady wares, exercised his vocation of a protector of society, and cultivated his domestic virtues. These last were pronounced.
He was thoroughly domesticated.
He found at home the ease of his body and the peace of his conscience, together with Mrs. Verloc's wifely attentions and Mrs. Verloc's mother's deferential regard.
In Winnie's mother's opinion, Mr. Verloc was a very nice gentleman.
Her son-in-law's heavy good nature inspired her with a sense of absolute safety.
Her daughter's future was obviously assured, and even as to her son Stevie she need have no anxiety.
She had not been able to conceal from herself that he was a terrible encumbrance, that poor Stevie.
But in view of Winnie's fondness for her delicate brother, and of Mr. Verloc's kind and generous disposition, she felt that the poor boy was pretty safe in this rough world.

Such was the house, the household, and the business Mr. Verloc left behind him on his way westward at half past ten in the morning. It was unusually early for him.
He surveyed the evidence of the town's opulence, approvingly. All these people had to be protected.
Protection is the first necessity of opulence and luxury. They had to be protected; and their horses, carriages, houses, servants, had to be protected; and the source of their wealth had to be protected in the heart of the city and the heart of the country; the whole social order favorable to their hygienic idleness had to be protected against the shallow enviousness of unhygienic labor.
It had to -- and Mr. Verloc would have rubbed his hands with satisfaction had he not been constitutionally averse from every superfluous exertion.

VERLOC.
Hurmpf
WE ARE NOT SATISFIED WITH THE ATTITUDE OF THE POLICE HERE. WHAT IS DESIRED IS THE OCCURRENCE OF SOMETHING WHICH SHOULD STIMULATE THEIR VIGILANCE.
"I THINK THAT YOU HAD BETTER SEE MR. VLADIMIR."
HOW LONG HAVE YOU BEEN EMPLOYED BY THE EMBASSY HERE?
"ELEVEN YEARS."
YOU DON'T SEEM TO BE VERY SMART--
WHAT WE WANT NOW IS ACTIVITY. YOU ARE AN AGENT PROVOCATEUR. THE BUSINESS OF A PROVOCATEUR IS TO PROVOKE.
"YOU HAVE DONE NOTHING TO EARN YOUR MONEY."
"NOTHING!? I HAVE SEVERAL TIMES PREVENTED WHAT--"
"DON'T BE ABSURD."
"WE DON'T WANT PREVENTION --WE WANT CURE. THAT WORTHLESS ANARCHIST ORGANIZATION, THE FUTURE OF THE PROLETARIAT. ARE YOU IN IT?"
"ONE OF THE VICE PRESIDENTS..."
"THEN YOU OUGHT TO BE ASHAMED OF YOURSELF! LOOK HERE. I TELL YOU PLAINLY THAT YOU WILL HAVE TO EARN YOUR MONEY. THE GOOD OLD DAYS ARE OVER. NO WORK, NO PAY."

This then was the famous and trusty secret agent, so secret that he was never designated otherwise than by the symbol Δ in the late Baron Stott-Wartenheim's official and confidential correspondence; the celebrated agent Δ whose warnings had the power to change the schemes and dates of royal, imperial, grandducal journeys, and sometimes cause them to be put off altogether!
His excellency had had social revolution on the brain. His prophetic and doleful dispatches had been for years the joke of foreign offices. He was said to have exclaimed on his deathbed: "Unhappied Europe! Thalt shalt perish by the moral insanity of thy children!" He was fated to be the victim of the first humbugging rascal that came along --
"WHAT WE WANT IS TO ADMINISTER A TONIC TO THE CONFERENCE IN MILAN. ITS DELIBERATIONS UPON INTERNATIONAL ACTION FOR THE SUPPRESSION OF INTERNATIONAL CRIME DON'T SEEM TO GET ANYWHERE."
"I SUPPOSE YOU AGREE THE MIDDLE CLASSES ARE STUPID?"
"THEY ARE."
"THEY HAVE NO IMAGINATION. THEY ARE BLINDED BY AN IDIOTIC VANITY. WHAT THEY WANT JUST NOW IS A JOLLY GOOD SCARE. THIS IS THE PSYCHOLOGICAL MOMENT TO SET YOUR ANARCHIST FRIENDS TO WORK.
"I HAVE HAD YOU CALLED HERE TO DEVELOP TO YOU MY IDEA.
"A SERIES OF OUTRAGES EXECUTED HERE IN THIS COUNTRY; NOT ONLY PLANNED HERE -- THAT WOULD NOT DO.
"THEY MUST BE SUFFICIENTLY STARTLING -- EFFECTIVE. LET THEM BE DIRECTED AGAINST BUILDINGS, FOR INSTANCE. WHAT IS THE FETISH OF THE HOUR THAT ALL THE BOURGEOIS RECOGNIZE -- EH, MR. VERLOC?"

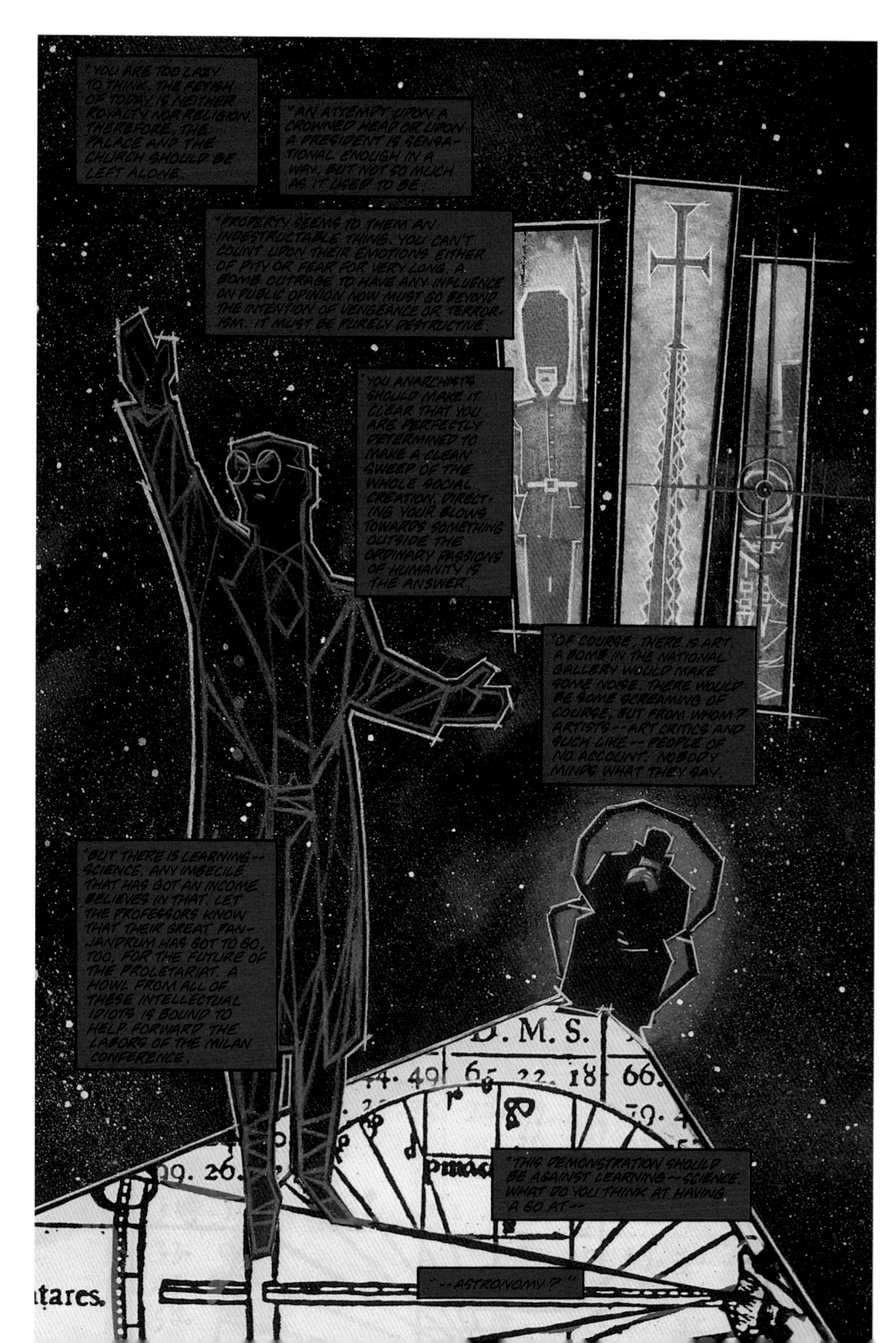
"YOU ARE TOO LAZY TO THINK. THE FETISH OF TODAY IS NEITHER ROYALTY NOR RELIGION. THEREFORE, THE PALACE AND THE CHURCH SHOULD BE LEFT ALONE.
"AN ATTEMPT UPON A CROWNED HEAD OR UPON A PRESIDENT IS SENSATIONAL ENOUGH IN A WAY, BUT NOT SO MUCH AS IT USED TO BE.
"PROPERTY SEEMS TO THEM AN INDESTRUCTABLE THING. YOU CAN'T COUNT UPON THEIR EMOTIONS EITHER OF PITY OR FEAR FOR VERY LONG. A BOMB OUTRAGE TO HAVE ANY INFLUENCE ON PUBLIC OPINION NOW MUST GO BEYOND THE INTENTION OF VENGEANCE OR TERRORISM. IT MUST BE PURELY DESTRUCTIVE.
"YOU ANARCHISTS SHOULD MAKE IT CLEAR THAT YOU ARE PERFECTLY DETERMINED TO MAKE A CLEAN SWEEP OF THE WHOLE SOCIAL CREATION, DIRECTING YOUR BLOWS TOWARDS SOMETHING OUTSIDE THE ORDINARY PASSIONS OF HUMANITY IS THE ANSWER.
"OF COURSE, THERE IS ART. A BOMB IN THE NATIONAL GALLERY WOULD MAKE SOME NOISE. THERE WOULD BE SOME SCREAMING OF COURSE, BUT FROM WHOM? ARTISTS -- ART CRITICS AND SUCH LIKE -- PEOPLE OF NO ACCOUNT. NOBODY MINDS WHAT THEY SAY.
"BUT THERE IS LEARNING -- SCIENCE. ANY IMBECILE THAT HAS GOT AN INCOME BELIEVES IN THAT. LET THE PROFESSORS KNOW THAT THEIR GREAT PANJANDRUM HAS GOT TO GO, TOO, FOR THE FUTURE OF THE PROLETARIAT. A HOWL FROM ALL OF THESE INTELLECTUAL IDIOTS IS BOUND TO HELP FORWARD THE LABORS OF THE MILAN CONFERENCE.
D. M. S.
"THIS DEMONSTRATION SHOULD BE AGAINST LEARNING -- SCIENCE. WHAT DO YOU THINK AT HAVING A GO AT --
"-- ASTRONOMY?"

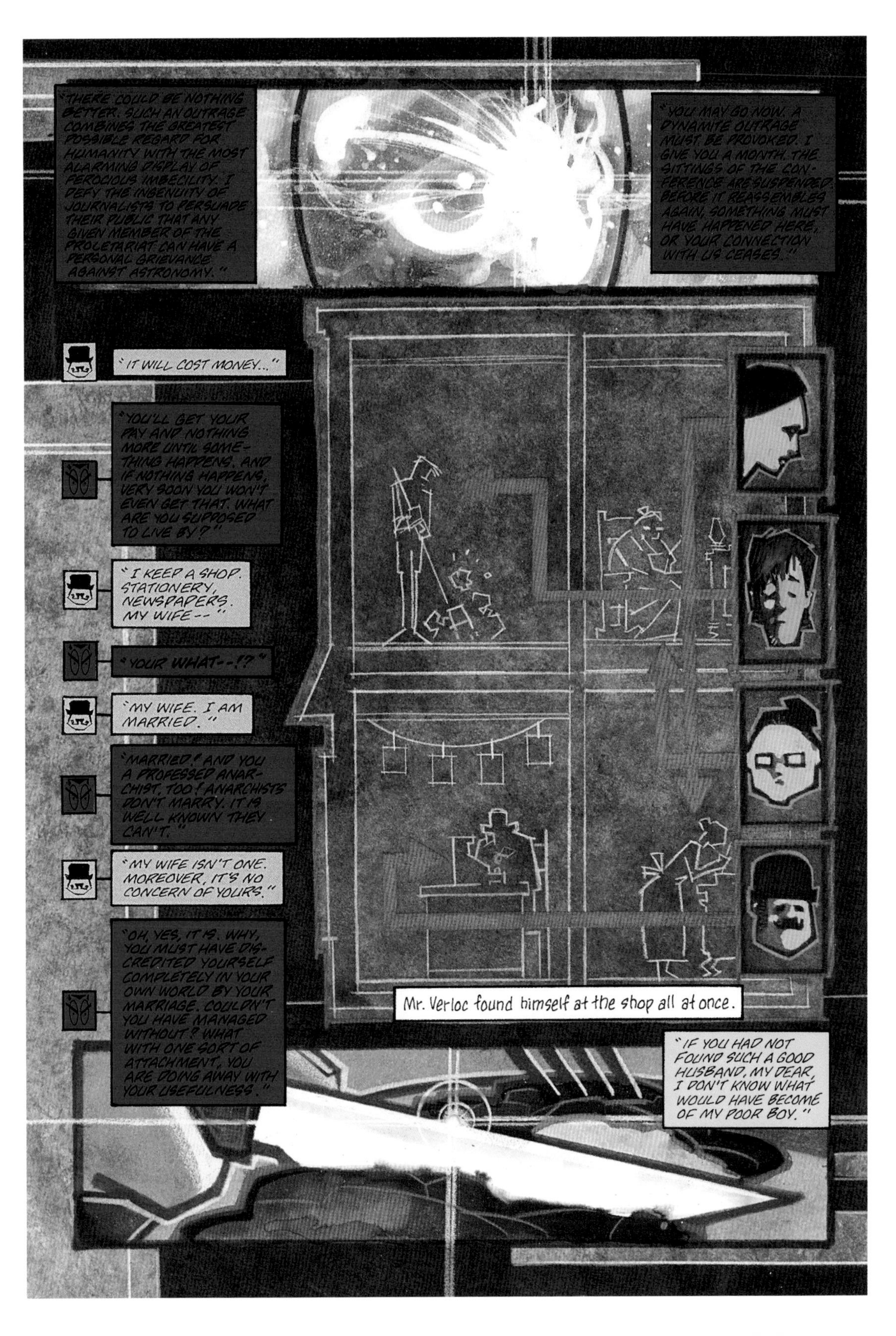
"THERE COULD BE NOTHING BETTER. SUCH AN OUTRAGE COMBINES THE GREATEST POSSIBLE REGARD FOR HUMANITY WITH THE MOST ALARMING DISPLAY OF FEROCIOUS IMBECILITY. I DEFY THE INGENUITY OF JOURNALISTS TO PERSUADE THEIR PUBLIC THAT ANY GIVEN MEMBER OF THE PROLETARIAT CAN HAVE A PERSONAL GRIEVANCE AGAINST ASTRONOMY."
"YOU MAY GO NOW. A DYNAMITE OUTRAGE MUST BE PROVOKED. I GIVE YOU A MONTH. THE SITTINGS OF THE CONFERENCE ARE SUSPENDED. BEFORE IT REASSEMBLES AGAIN, SOMETHING MUST HAVE HAPPENED HERE, OR YOUR CONNECTION WITH US CEASES."
"IT WILL COST MONEY..."
"YOU'LL GET YOUR PAY AND NOTHING MORE UNTIL SOMETHING HAPPENS. AND IF NOTHING HAPPENS, VERY SOON YOU WON'T EVEN GET THAT. WHAT ARE YOU SUPPOSED TO LIVE BY?"
"I KEEP A SHOP. STATIONERY, NEWSPAPERS. MY WIFE--"
"YOUR WHAT--!?"
"MY WIFE. I AM MARRIED."
"MARRIED! AND YOU A PROFESSED ANARCHIST, TOO! ANARCHISTS DON'T MARRY. IT IS WELL KNOWN THEY CAN'T."
"MY WIFE ISN'T ONE. MOREOVER, IT'S NO CONCERN OF YOURS."
"OH, YES, IT IS. WHY, YOU MUST HAVE DISCREDITED YOURSELF COMPLETELY IN YOUR OWN WORLD BY YOUR MARRIAGE. COULDN'T YOU HAVE MANAGED WITHOUT? WHAT WITH ONE SORT OF ATTACHMENT, YOU ARE DOING AWAY WITH YOUR USEFULNESS."
Mr. Verloc found himself at the shop all at once.
"IF YOU HAD NOT FOUND SUCH A GOOD HUSBAND, MY DEAR, I DON'T KNOW WHAT WOULD HAVE BECOME OF MY POOR BOY."

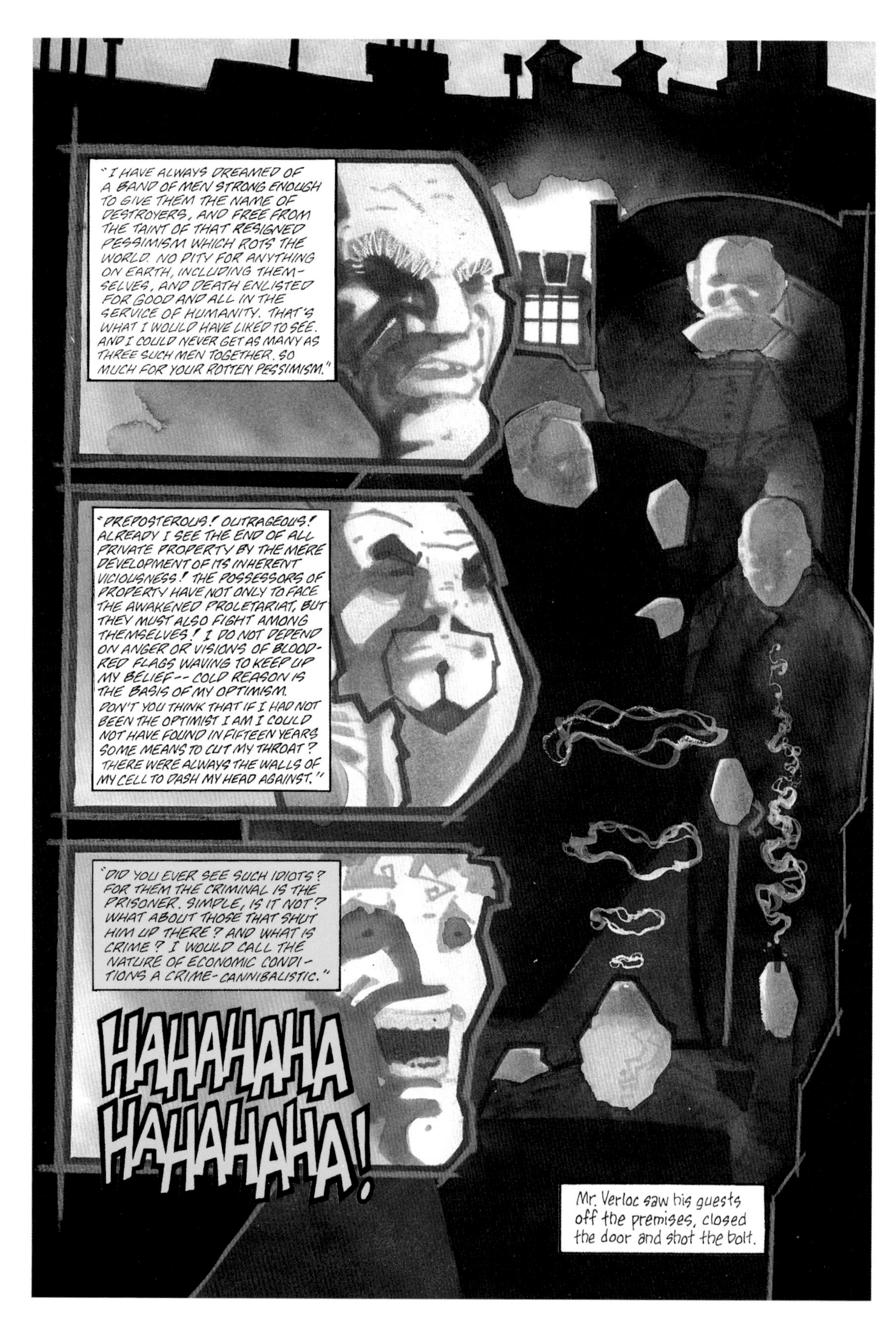
"I HAVE ALWAYS DREAMED OF A BAND OF MEN STRONG ENOUGH TO GIVE THEM THE NAME OF DESTROYERS, AND FREE FROM THE TAINT OF THAT RESIGNED PESSIMISM WHICH ROTS THE WORLD. NO PITY FOR ANYTHING ON EARTH, INCLUDING THEMSELVES, AND DEATH ENLISTED FOR GOOD AND ALL IN THE SERVICE OF HUMANITY. THAT'S WHAT I WOULD HAVE LIKED TO SEE. AND I COULD NEVER GET AS MANY AS THREE SUCH MEN TOGETHER. SO MUCH FOR YOUR ROTTEN PESSIMISM."
"PREPOSTEROUS! OUTRAGEOUS! ALREADY I SEE THE END OF ALL PRIVATE PROPERTY BY THE MERE DEVELOPMENT OF ITS INHERENT VICIOUSNESS! THE POSSESSORS OF PROPERTY HAVE NOT ONLY TO FACE THE AWAKENED PROLETARIAT, BUT THEY MUST ALSO FIGHT AMONG THEMSELVES! I DO NOT DEPEND ON ANGER OR VISIONS OF BLOOD-RED FLAGS WAVING TO KEEP UP MY BELIEF-- COLD REASON IS THE BASIS OF MY OPTIMISM. DON'T YOU THINK THAT IF I HAD NOT BEEN THE OPTIMIST I AM I COULD NOT HAVE FOUND IN FIFTEEN YEARS SOME MEANS TO CUT MY THROAT? THERE WERE ALWAYS THE WALLS OF MY CELL TO DASH MY HEAD AGAINST."
"DID YOU EVER SEE SUCH IDIOTS? FOR THEM THE CRIMINAL IS THE PRISONER. SIMPLE, IS IT NOT? WHAT ABOUT THOSE THAT SHUT HIM UP THERE? AND WHAT IS CRIME? I WOULD CALL THE NATURE OF ECONOMIC CONDITIONS A CRIME- CANNIBALISTIC."
HAHAHAHA HAHAHAHA!
Mr. Verloc saw his guests off the premises, closed the door and shot the bolt.

Pausing in his intention to turn off the gas, Mr. Verloc descended into the abyss of moral reflections.
A lazy lot--this Karl Yundt, nursed by a bleary-eyed old woman he had years ago enticed away from a friend.
As to Ossipon, that beggar was sure to want for nothing as long as there were silly girls with savings bank-books in the world.
Mr. Verloc's morality was offended also by the optimism of Michaelis, kept but lately annexed by a wealthy old lady to a country cottage.
Loafing was all very well for these fellows, who knew not the dangerous Mr. Vladimir and had women to fall back on...

At this point, Mr. Verloc was brought face to face with the necessity of going to bed some time or other that evening. Then why not go now--? The necessity was not so normally pleasurable as it ought to have been for a man of his age and temperament.
He dreaded the demon of sleeplessness, which he felt had marked him for its own.
THE ILLUSTRATED POLICE NEWS
He had gone into trade for no commercial reasons. He was guided in the selection of this peculiar line of business by a distinctive leaning towards shady transactions, where money is picked up easily. Moreover, it did not take him out of his sphere.
On the contrary, it gave him a publicly confessed standing in that sphere, and Mr. Verloc had unconfessed relations which made him familiar with, yet careless of, the police. There was a distinct advantage in such a situation. But as a means of livelihood it was by itself insufficient.
I DON'T FEEL VERY WELL.
NOT AT ALL WELL.
I HAVEN'T BEEN FEELING WELL FOR THE LAST FEW DAYS.

"THAT BOY HEARS TOO MUCH OF WHAT IS TALKED ABOUT HERE. IF I HAD KNOWN... HE WAS OUT OF HIS MIND WITH SOMETHING HE HAD OVER-HEARD ABOUT EATING PEOPLE'S FLESH. WHAT'S THAT?"
"ASK KARL YUNDT."
...disgusting old man...
Mr. Verloc felt the latent unfriendliness of all out of doors with a force approaching positive bodily anguish. There is no occupation that fails a man more completely than that of a secret agent of the police.
YOU'LL CATCH COLD STANDING THERE.

DID YOU TURN OFF THE GAS DOWNSTAIRS?

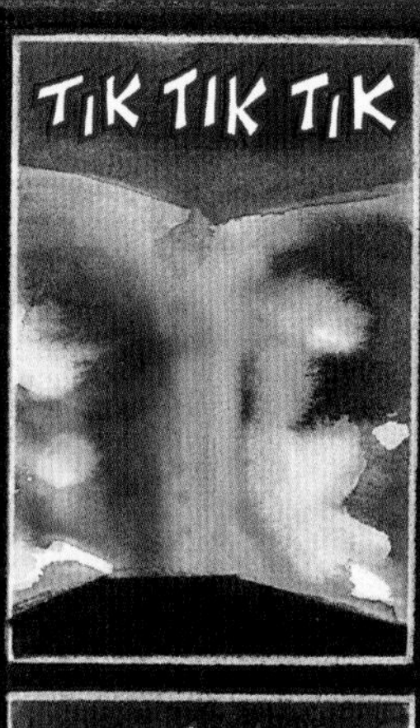
TIK TIK TIK

YES, I DID. THAT BOY IS IN A VERY EXCITED STATE TONIGHT.

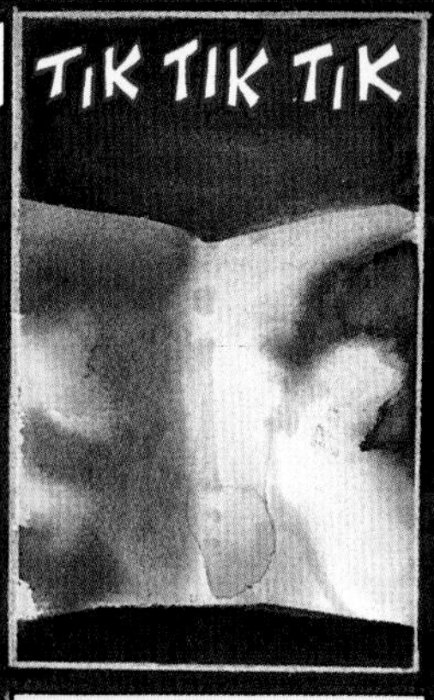
TIK TIK TIK

STEVIE ISN'T FIT TO HEAR WHAT'S TALKED ABOUT HERE.

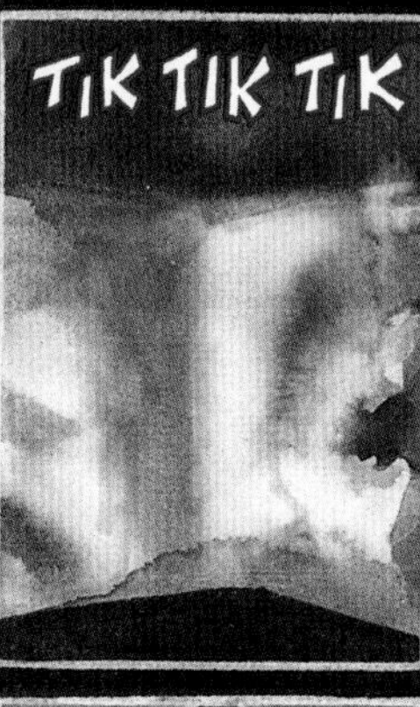
TIK TIK TIK

HE BELIEVES IT'S TRUE. I WISH HE HAD NEVER BEEN TO SCHOOL.

"HE'S ALWAYS TAKING THE NEWSPAPERS FROM THE WINDOW TO READ. THERE WAS A STORY OF A GERMAN OFFICER TEARING HALF THE EAR OFF OF A RE-CRUIT! I COULDN'T DO ANYTHING WITH STEVIE THAT AFTERNOON!"

"I HAD TO TAKE THE CARVING KNIFE FROM THE BOY! HE CAN'T STAND THE NOTION OF ANY CRUELTY.

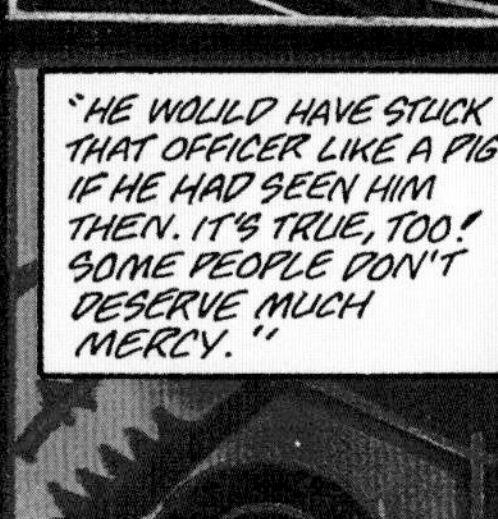
"HE WOULD HAVE STUCK THAT OFFICER LIKE A PIG IF HE HAD SEEN HIM THEN. IT'S TRUE, TOO! SOME PEOPLE DON'T DESERVE MUCH MERCY."

I'M GOING ON THE CONTINENT TOMORROW. FOR A FEW WEEKS.

Oh. SHALL I PUT THE LIGHT OUT?

TIK TIK TIK

YES, PUT IT OUT.

TIK TIK TIK

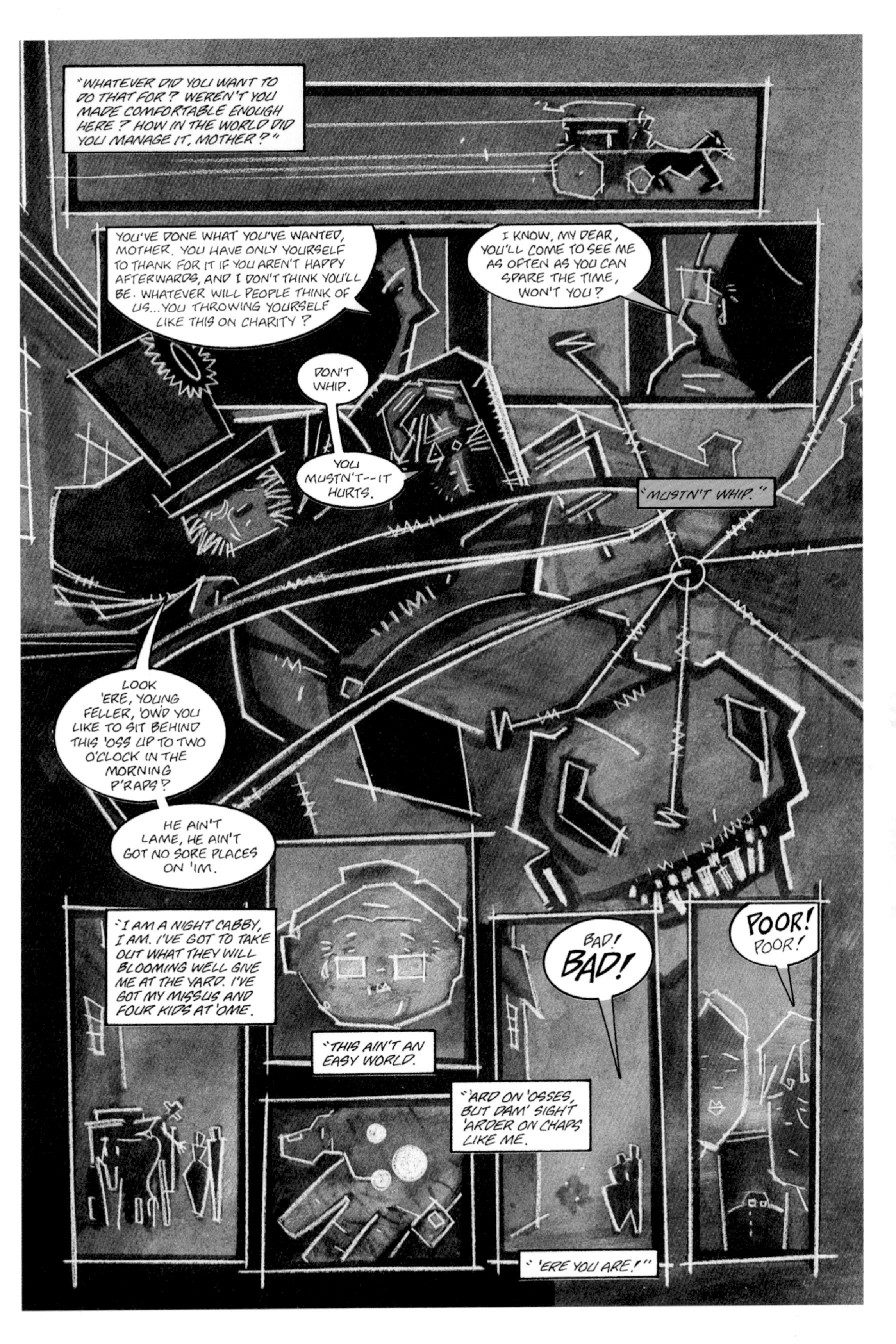

"WHATEVER DID YOU WANT TO DO THAT FOR? WEREN'T YOU MADE COMFORTABLE ENOUGH HERE? HOW IN THE WORLD DID YOU MANAGE IT, MOTHER?"
YOU'VE DONE WHAT YOU'VE WANTED, MOTHER. YOU HAVE ONLY YOURSELF TO THANK FOR IT IF YOU AREN'T HAPPY AFTERWARDS, AND I DON'T THINK YOU'LL BE. WHATEVER WILL PEOPLE THINK OF US...YOU THROWING YOURSELF LIKE THIS ON CHARITY?
I KNOW, MY DEAR, YOU'LL COME TO SEE ME AS OFTEN AS YOU CAN SPARE THE TIME, WON'T YOU?
DON'T WHIP.
YOU MUSTN'T--IT HURTS.
"MUSTN'T WHIP."
LOOK 'ERE, YOUNG FELLER, 'OW'D YOU LIKE TO SIT BEHIND THIS 'OSS UP TO TWO O'CLOCK IN THE MORNING P'RAPS?
HE AIN'T LAME, HE AIN'T GOT NO SORE PLACES ON 'IM.
"I AM A NIGHT CABBY, I AM. I'VE GOT TO TAKE OUT WHAT THEY WILL BLOOMING WELL GIVE ME AT THE YARD. I'VE GOT MY MISSUS AND FOUR KIDS AT 'OME.
"THIS AIN'T AN EASY WORLD.
"'ARD ON 'OSSES, BUT DAM' SIGHT 'ARDER ON CHAPS LIKE ME.
BAD! BAD!
POOR! POOR!
"'ERE YOU ARE!"

BAD WORLD FOR POOR PEOPLE

"NOW, STEVIE, YOU MUST LOOK WELL AFTER ME AT THE CROSSINGS, AND GET FIRST INTO THE BUS, LIKE A GOOD BROTHER."

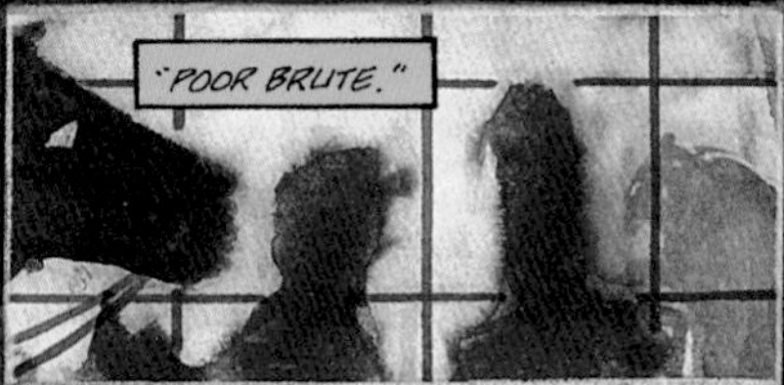

"POOR BRUTE."

POOR! POOR!

POOR BRUTE, POOR PEOPLE!

"SHAME!"

"COME ALONG, STEVIE. YOU CAN'T HELP THAT."

Somebody, he felt, ought to be punished for it-- punished with great severity.

"POLICE."

"THE POLICE AREN'T FOR THAT, STEVIE."

"WHAT ARE THEY FOR THEN, WINN? WHAT ARE THEY FOR? TELL ME."

"THE POLICE ARE THERE SO THAT THEM AS HAVE NOTHING SHOULDN'T TAKE ANYTHING AWAY FROM THEM WHO HAVE."

"WHAT? NOT EVEN IF THEY WERE HUNGRY? MUSTN'T THEY?"

"CERTAINLY NOT. BUT WHAT'S THE USE OF TALKING ABOUT ALL THAT? YOU AREN'T EVER HUNGRY-- QUICK, STEVIE, STOP THAT GREEN BUS."

Mr. Verloc, returning from the continent, brought back a mind unfreshened by travel.
I WISH YOU'D TAKE THAT BOY OUT WITH YOU, ADOLF.
HE'LL GET LOST IN THE STREET.
HE WON'T. THAT BOY JUST WORSHIPS YOU.
WELL, LET HIM COME ALONG THEN.
He entered the shop with an air of sombre exhaustion.
MIGHT BE FATHER AND SON.

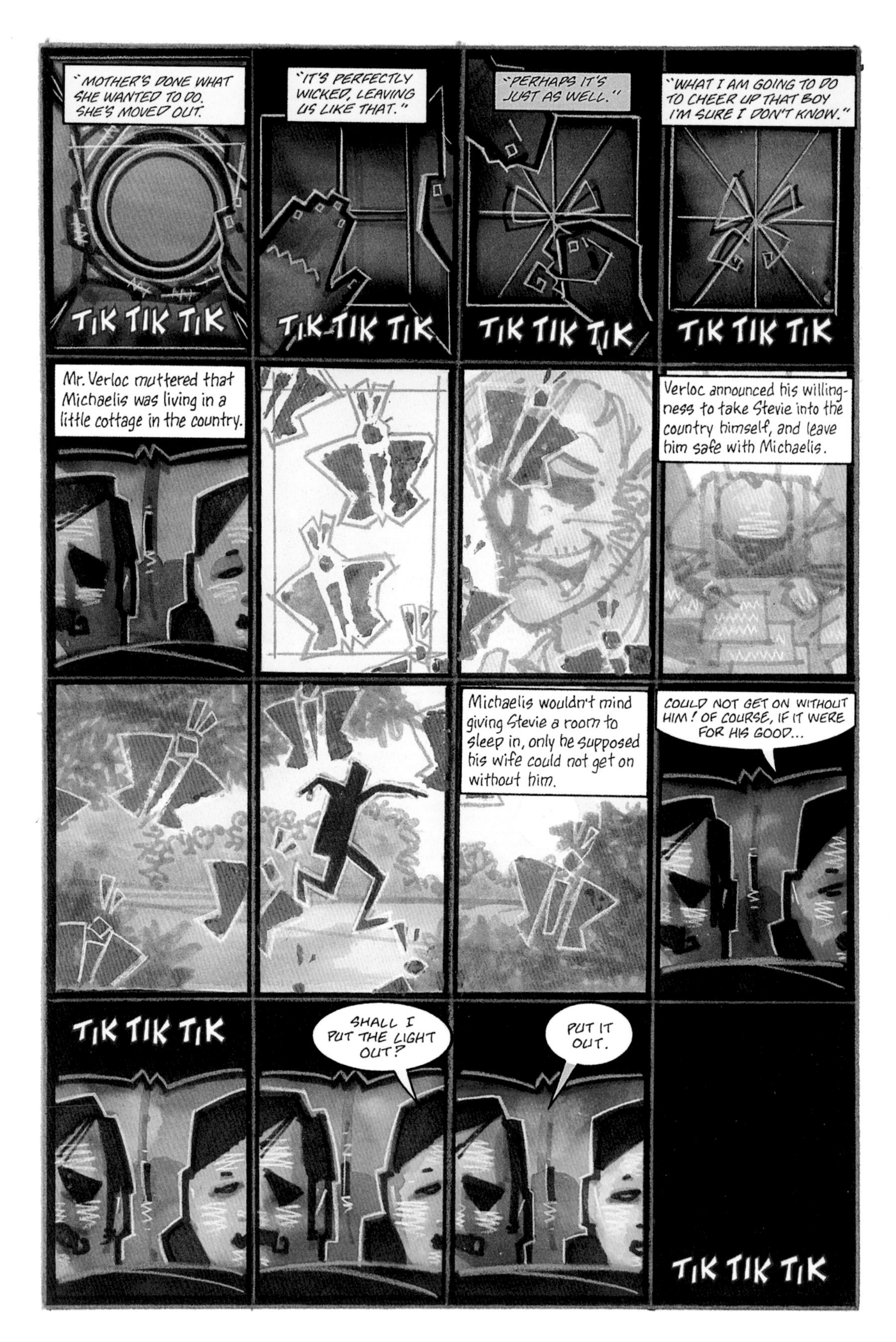
"MOTHER'S DONE WHAT SHE WANTED TO DO. SHE'S MOVED OUT.
TIK TIK TIK
"IT'S PERFECTLY WICKED, LEAVING US LIKE THAT."
TIK TIK TIK
"PERHAPS IT'S JUST AS WELL."
TIK TIK TIK
"WHAT I AM GOING TO DO TO CHEER UP THAT BOY I'M SURE I DON'T KNOW."
TIK TIK TIK
Mr. Verloc muttered that Michaelis was living in a little cottage in the country.
Verloc announced his willingness to take Stevie into the country himself, and leave him safe with Michaelis.
Michaelis wouldn't mind giving Stevie a room to sleep in, only he supposed his wife could not get on without him.
COULD NOT GET ON WITHOUT HIM! OF COURSE, IF IT WERE FOR HIS GOOD...
TIK TIK TIK
SHALL I PUT THE LIGHT OUT?
PUT IT OUT.
TIK TIK TIK

TIK TIK TIK TI*

"BEEN SITTING LONG HERE?"
"AN HOUR OR MORE."
"YOU HAVEN'T HEARD YET THE NEWS, HAVE YOU? IT'S WONDERFUL YOU OF ALL PEOPLE HAVE HEARD NOTHING OF IT. DO YOU --GIVE YOUR STUFF TO ANYBODY WHO ASKS FOR IT?"
"MY ABSOLUTE RULE IS NEVER TO REFUSE ANYBODY--AS LONG AS I HAVE A PINCH BY ME. WHY SHOULD I THINK TWICE ABOUT IT?"
THEY COULD SEND SOMEONE-- RIG A PLANT ON YOU. DON'T YOU SEE? GET THE STUFF FROM YOU IN THAT WAY, AND THEN ARREST YOU WITH THE PROOF IN THEIR HANDS.
PROOF OF WHAT? DEALING IN EXPLOSIVES WITHOUT A LICENSE PERHAPS. I DON'T THINK THERE'S ONE OF THEM ANXIOUS TO MAKE THAT ARREST.
"WHY?"
"BECAUSE THEY KNOW I TAKE CARE NEVER TO PART WITH THE LAST OF MY WARES.
"I SHALL NEVER BE ARRESTED. THE GAME ISN'T GOOD ENOUGH FOR ANY POLICEMAN. TO DEAL WITH A MAN LIKE ME REQUIRES SHEER, NAKED, INGLORIOUS HEROISM."
"OR RECKLESSNESS-- OR SIMPLY IGNORANCE. THEY'VE ONLY TO GET SOMEBODY WHO DOES NOT KNOW YOU CARRY ENOUGH STUFF TO BLOW YOURSELF AND EVERYTHING NEAR YOU TO PIECES."
"I NEVER AFFIRMED I COULD NOT BE ELIMINATED. BUT THAT WOULDN'T BE AN ARREST. MOREOVER, IT'S NOT AS EASY AS IT LOOKS."
"BAH! DON'T BE TOO SURE OF THAT. WHAT'S TO PREVENT HALF A DOZEN OF THEM FROM JUMPING YOU AND PINNING YOUR ARMS? YOU COULD DO NOTHING --COULD YOU?"
"YES, I COULD. THE DETONATOR IS PARTLY MECHANICAL, PARTLY CHEMICAL."
"IT IS INSTANTANEOUS?"
1 · 2 · 3 · 4 · 5 · 6 · 7 · 8 · 9 · 10 · 11 · 12 · 13 · 14 · 15 · 16 · 17 · 18 · 19 · 20
"FAR FROM IT. A FULL TWENTY SECONDS MUST ELAPSE FROM THE MOMENT I PRESS THE BALL TILL THE EXPLOSION TAKES PLACE."
"TWENTY SECONDS! HORRORS!
"NOBODY IN THIS ROOM COULD HOPE TO ESCAPE.
"IN THE LAST INSTANCE IT IS CHARACTER ALONE THAT MAKES FOR ONE'S SAFETY."
"I WONDER HOW YOU MANAGED IT."
"FORCE OF PERSONALITY."

"YOU REVOLUTIONISTS-- ARE SLAVES OF THE SOCIAL CONVENTION, WHICH IS AFRAID OF YOU; SLAVES AS MUCH AS THE POLICE THAT STAND UP IN DEFENSE OF THAT CONVENTION. CLEARLY YOU ARE, SINCE YOU WANT TO REVOLUTIONIZE IT."
"THEN WHAT DO YOU WANT FROM US? WHAT IS IT YOU ARE AFTER YOURSELF?"
"A PERFECT DETONATOR.
"WHAT ARE YOU MAKING THAT FACE FOR? YOU CANNOT EVEN BEAR THE MENTION OF SOMETHING CONCLUSIVE.
"THE TERRORIST AND POLICEMAN BOTH COME FROM THE SAME BASKET. REVOLUTION, LEGALITY-- COUNTER-MOVES IN THE SAME GAME.
"BUT I DON'T PLAY; I WORK FOURTEEN HOURS A DAY, AND SOMETIMES GO HUNGRY. I'VE THE GRIT TO WORK ALONE. I'VE WORKED ALONE FOR YEARS."
AT THE PERFECT DETONATOR, EH?
A PERFECT DEFINITION. YOU COULDN'T FIND ANYTHING SO PRECISE TO DEFINE THE NATURE OF YOUR ACTIVITY WITH ALL OF YOUR COMMITTEES AND DELEGATIONS.
IT IS I WHO AM THE TRUE PROPAGANDIST.
"WE WON'T DISCUSS THAT POINT. I AM AFRAID I'LL HAVE TO SPOIL YOUR HOLIDAY FOR YOU, THOUGH. HERE. SEE?"
BOMB IN GREENWICH PARK
"ARE YOU REALLY HANDING YOUR STUFF OVER TO THE FIRST FOOL WHO COMES ALONG?"
"I WOULD SHOVEL MY STUFF IN HEAPS IN THE STREETS IF I HAD ENOUGH. AS I HAVEN'T, I DO MY BEST BY PERFECTING A DEPENDABLE DETONATOR."
YES, YOUR DETONATORS. I WONDER IF IT WEREN'T ONE OF YOUR DETONATORS THAT MADE A CLEAN SWEEP OF THE MAN IN THE PARK. WHO COULD THAT FELLOW BE?
WELL, I DON'T THINK THERE CAN BE THE SLIGHTEST OBJECTION NOW--
--VERLOC.
"HALF PAST ELEVEN. FOGGY MORNING."
"A MAN'S BODY BLOWN TO PIECES. A WICKED ATTEMPT TO BLOW UP THE OBSERVATORY, THEY SAY, BUT HARDLY CREDIBLE. THE FRAGMENTS OF ONLY ONE MAN-- ERGO-- BLEW HIMSELF UP."
"I HADN'T THE SLIGHTEST IDEA OF ANYTHING OF THE SORT BEING PLANNED. THIS MAY AFFECT US VERY ADVERSELY IN THIS COUNTRY."
IMPOSSIBLE!

"YES. HE'S THE PERSON. YOU CAN'T SAY I WAS GIVING MY STUFF TO THE FIRST FOOL WHO CAME ALONG. HE WAS A PROMINENT MEMBER OF YOUR GROUP, I UNDERSTAND."

"NOT EXACTLY. HE WAS THE CENTER FOR GENERAL INTELLIGENCE, AND USUALLY RECEIVED COMRADES COMING OVER HERE. MORE USEFUL THAN IMPORTANT. MAN OF NO IDEAS.

"THE ONLY TALENT HE SHOWED REALLY WAS HIS ABILITY TO ELUDE THE POLICE.

"HE WAS REGULARLY MARRIED, YOU KNOW. I SUPPOSE IT'S WITH HER MONEY THAT HE STARTED THE SHOP."

"I WONDER WHAT THAT WOMAN WILL DO NOW? INTEL-LECTUALLY, A NON-ENTITY. QUITE AN ORDINARY PERSONALITY."

"YOU ARE WRONG IN NOT KEEPING MORE IN TOUCH WITH THE COMRADES, PROFESSOR. DID HE GIVE YOU SOME IDEA OF HIS INTENTIONS?"

"HE TOLD ME IT WAS GOING TO BE A DEMONSTRATION AGAINST A BUILDING. AS HE WANTED SOMETHING THAT COULD BE CARRIED OPENLY IN THE HAND, I PROPOSED TO MAKE USE OF AN OLD VARNISH CAN. IT WAS INGENIOUS--A COMBINATION OF TIME AND SHOCK."

"WHAT DO YOU THINK HAS HAPPENED?"

"CAN'T TELL. THE CONTACT WAS MADE ALL RIGHT--THAT'S CLEAR TO ME AT ANY RATE."

NO DOUBT THE POLICE ARE AWARE WELL ENOUGH THAT WE HAD NOTHING TO DO WITH THIS--WHAT THEY WILL SAY IS ANOTHER THING.
CONFOUNDED ASS!
I WONDER WHAT I HAD BETTER DO NOW?

"FASTEN YOURSELF UPON THE WOMAN FOR ALL SHE IS WORTH."

Leaving Ossipon startled, the Professor walked out. He turned brusquely into a narrow alley.
HALLO!
NOT IN A HURRY TO GET HOME?
It was in reality a chance meeting. Chief Inspector Heat had had a disagreeably busy day since his department received the first telegram from Greenwich a little before eleven in the morning. He had missed his breakfast.
First of all, the fact of the outrage being attempted less than a week after he had assured the Assistant Commissioner that no outbreak of anarchist activity was to be apprehended was sufficiently annoying.
Starting immediately to begin his investigation on the spot, he had walked to the hospital.
There he had examined the remains. When he had finished he had lost all inclination for food.

It was in this mental disposition, still nauseated, that Inspector Heat had come upon the professor.
YOU ARE NOT WANTED. NOT YET.
WHEN I WANT YOU, I WILL TELL YOU.
I'VE NO DOUBT THE PAPERS WOULD GIVE YOU AN OBITUARY NOTICE THEN. YOU MAY BE EXPOSED TO THE UNPLEASANTNESS OF BEING BURIED TOGETHER WITH ME, THOUGH I SUPPOSE YOUR FRIENDS WOULD MAKE AN EFFORT TO SORT US OUT.
"ALL THIS IS GOOD TO FRIGHTEN CHILDREN WITH -- I'LL HAVE YOU YET."
"DOUBTLESS-- BUT THERE'S NO TIME LIKE THE PRESENT. THIS IS A FINE OPPORTUNITY FOR SELF SACRIFICE. THERE ISN'T EVEN A CAT NEAR US, AND THESE CONDEMNED OLD HOUSES WOULD MAKE A GOOD HEAD OF BRICKS WHERE YOU STAND. YOU'LL NEVER GET ME AT SO LITTLE COST TO LIFE AND PROPERTY, WHICH YOU ARE PAID TO PROTECT."
"IF I WERE TO LAY MY HANDS ON YOU NOW I WOULD BE NO BETTER THAN YOURSELF."
"AH! THE GAME!"
"YOU MAY BE SURE OUR SIDE WILL WIN IN THE END. IT MAY YET BE NECESSARY TO MAKE PEOPLE BELIEVE THAT SOME OF YOU OUGHT TO BE SHOT LIKE MAD DOGS. THEN THAT WILL BE THE GAME. BUT I'LL BE DAMNED IF I KNOW WHAT YOURS IS. I DON'T BELIEVE YOU KNOW YOURSELVES. YOU'LL NEVER GET ANYTHING BY IT."
"WHAT ARE YOU AFTER, THEN?"
"MEANTIME, IT'S YOU WHO GET SOMETHING FROM IT-- SO FAR. I WON'T SPEAK OF YOUR SALARY, BUT HAVEN'T YOU MADE YOUR NAME SIMPLY BY NOT UNDERSTANDING WHAT WE ARE AFTER?"
GIVE IT UP-- WHATEVER IT IS. YOU'LL FIND WE ARE TOO MANY FOR YOU.
DON'T BELIEVE ME... EH? WE ARE. AND ANYWAY, YOU'RE ALWAYS MAKING A MESS OF IT. WHY, IF THIEVES DIDN'T KNOW THEIR WORK ANY BETTER THEY WOULD STARVE.
"I AM DOING MY WORK BETTER THAN YOU ARE DOING YOURS."
LUNATIC.

Upon returning to headquarters, the Chief Inspector was admitted at once to the Assistant Commissioner's private room.
"YOU BELIEVE THERE WERE TWO MEN?"
THE CORONER'S JURY WILL HAVE A TREAT.
WE SHALL HAVE NOTHING TO TELL THEM.
THE PORTER WHO TOOK THE TICKETS AT MAZE HILL REMEMBERS TWO CHAPS ANSWERING TO THE DESCRIPTION PASSING THE BARRIER.
THEY SEEMED TO HIM TWO RESPECTABLE WORKING MEN... SIGN PAINTERS OR HOUSE DECORATORS.
THE BIG MAN GOT OUT OF A THIRD CLASS COMPARTMENT BACKWARD, WITH A BRIGHT TIN CAN IN HIS HAND. ON THE PLATFORM HE GAVE IT TO THE FAIR YOUNG FELLOW WHO FOLLOWED HIM.
The Chief Inspector thought it more than probable. Taking the time those two men were seen coming out of Maze Hill station by an old woman, and the time when the explosion was heard, he thought the other man might have been actually at the Greenwich Park station, at the moment his comrade was destroying himself so thoroughly.
"AND THESE MEN CAME FROM THAT LITTLE COUNTRY STATION. TWO FOREIGN ANARCHISTS COMING FROM THAT PLACE. IT'S RATHER UNACCOUNTABLE."
"VERY THOROUGHLY, EH?"
"YES, SIR. IT WOULD BE STILL MORE UNACCOUNTABLE IF THAT MICHAELIS WEREN'T STAYING IN A COTTAGE IN THE NEIGHBORHOOD."
YOU CONNECT MICHAELIS WITH THIS AFFAIR? YOU WILL WANT SOME CONCLUSIVE EVIDENCE.

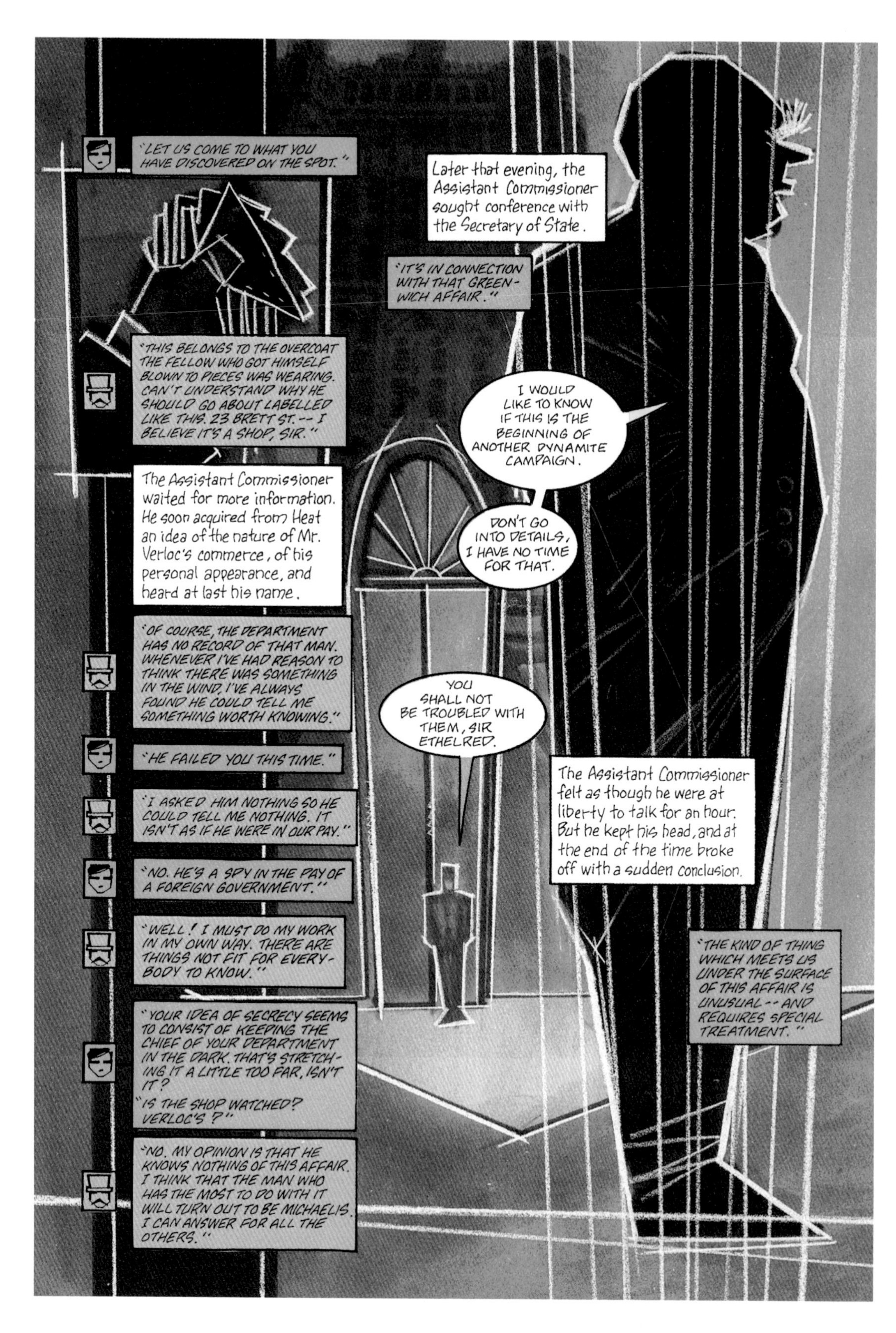
"LET US COME TO WHAT YOU HAVE DISCOVERED ON THE SPOT."
"THIS BELONGS TO THE OVERCOAT THE FELLOW WHO GOT HIMSELF BLOWN TO PIECES WAS WEARING. CAN'T UNDERSTAND WHY HE SHOULD GO ABOUT LABELLED LIKE THIS. 23 BRETT ST. -- I BELIEVE IT'S A SHOP, SIR."
The Assistant Commissioner waited for more information. He soon acquired from Heat an idea of the nature of Mr. Verloc's commerce, of his personal appearance, and heard at last his name.
"OF COURSE, THE DEPARTMENT HAS NO RECORD OF THAT MAN. WHENEVER I'VE HAD REASON TO THINK THERE WAS SOMETHING IN THE WIND, I'VE ALWAYS FOUND HE COULD TELL ME SOMETHING WORTH KNOWING."
"HE FAILED YOU THIS TIME."
"I ASKED HIM NOTHING SO HE COULD TELL ME NOTHING. IT ISN'T AS IF HE WERE IN OUR PAY."
"NO. HE'S A SPY IN THE PAY OF A FOREIGN GOVERNMENT."
"WELL! I MUST DO MY WORK IN MY OWN WAY. THERE ARE THINGS NOT FIT FOR EVERYBODY TO KNOW."
"YOUR IDEA OF SECRECY SEEMS TO CONSIST OF KEEPING THE CHIEF OF YOUR DEPARTMENT IN THE DARK. THAT'S STRETCHING IT A LITTLE TOO FAR, ISN'T IT?
"IS THE SHOP WATCHED? VERLOC'S?"
"NO. MY OPINION IS THAT HE KNOWS NOTHING OF THIS AFFAIR. I THINK THAT THE MAN WHO HAS THE MOST TO DO WITH IT WILL TURN OUT TO BE MICHAELIS. I CAN ANSWER FOR ALL THE OTHERS."
Later that evening, the Assistant Commissioner sought conference with the Secretary of State.
"IT'S IN CONNECTION WITH THAT GREENWICH AFFAIR."
I WOULD LIKE TO KNOW IF THIS IS THE BEGINNING OF ANOTHER DYNAMITE CAMPAIGN.
DON'T GO INTO DETAILS, I HAVE NO TIME FOR THAT.
YOU SHALL NOT BE TROUBLED WITH THEM, SIR ETHELRED.
The Assistant Commissioner felt as though he were at liberty to talk for an hour. But he kept his head, and at the end of the time broke off with a sudden conclusion.
"THE KIND OF THING WHICH MEETS US UNDER THE SURFACE OF THIS AFFAIR IS UNUSUAL -- AND REQUIRES SPECIAL TREATMENT."

"I SHOULD THINK SO-- INVOLVING THE AMBASSADOR OF A FOREIGN POWER!"
"YOU FORGET, SIR ETHELRED, THAT STRICTLY SPEAKING WE KNOW NOTHING POSITIVELY -- AS OF YET."
"BUT HOW WOULD YOU DEFINE IT? SHORTLY."
"BAREFACED AUDACITY AMOUNTING TO CHILDISHNESS OF A PECULIAR SORT."
"THEY'LL HAVE TO GET A HARD RAP ON THE KNUCKLES OVER THIS AFFAIR. WHAT IS YOUR GENERAL IDEA, STATED SHORTLY? NO NEED TO GO INTO DETAILS."
"I WAS REALLY THINKING THAT IT MIGHT BE BETTER AT THIS STAGE FOR INSPECTOR HEAT TO BE REPLACED BY--"
"WHY NOT LEAVE IT TO HEAT?"
"BECAUSE HE IS AN OLD DEPARTMENTAL HAND. THEY HAVE THEIR OWN MORALITY. MY LINE OF INQUIRY WOULD APPEAR TO HIM AN AWFUL PERVERSION OF DUTY. HE'S AN EXCELLENT SERVANT. WE MUST NOT PUT AN UNDUE STRAIN ON HIS LOYALTY. BESIDES, I WANT A FREE HAND-- A FREER HAND THAN IT WOULD BE PERHAPS ADVISABLE TO GIVE INSPECTOR HEAT."
CERTAINLY, FIND OUT AS MUCH AS YOU CAN; FIND IT OUT YOUR OWN WAY.
I MUST SET ABOUT IT WITHOUT LOSS OF TIME, THIS VERY EVENING.
COME TO THE HOUSE WITH YOUR DISCOVERIES. I'LL WARN TOODLES TO LOOK OUT FOR YOU.
I SHALL CERTAINLY BRING MY DISCOVERIES TO THE HOUSE ON THE CHANCE OF YOU HAVING THE TIME TO--
"I WON'T HAVE THE TIME, BUT I WILL SEE YOU."
The Assistant Commissioner dispatched a note to his wife, explaining that he would be absent from dinner that evening.

His descent into the street was like the descent into a slimy aquarium. He came to stand on the edge of the pavement and waited for a hansom. In this immoral atmosphere, the Assistant Commissioner, reflecting upon his enterprise, seemed to lose his identity.
It was not a long drive. He ordered in a little Italian restaurant.
He had a sense of loneliness, of evil freedom. It was rather pleasant.
Twenty-three Brett Street was not very far away.

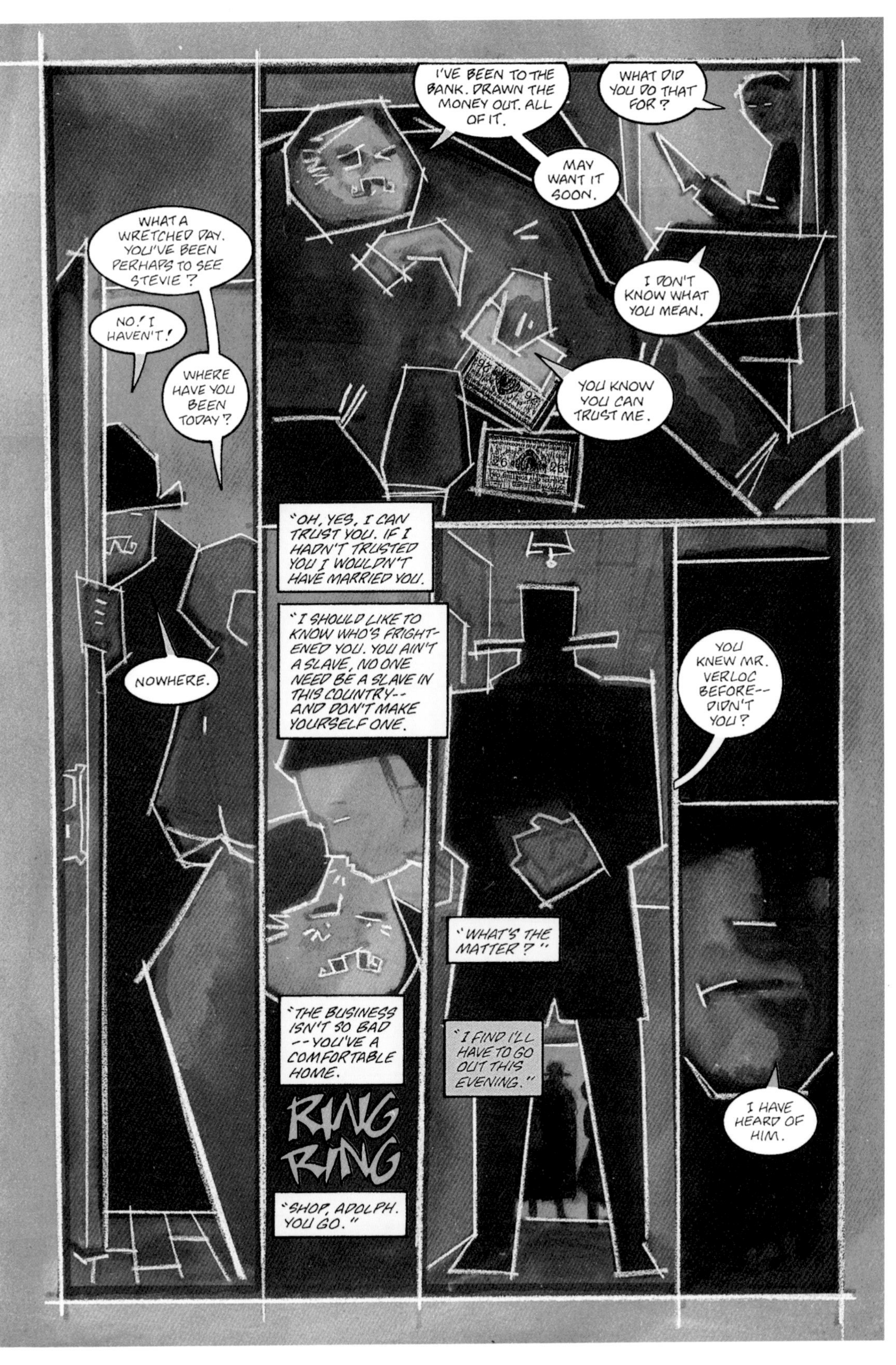

WHAT A WRETCHED DAY. YOU'VE BEEN PERHAPS TO SEE STEVIE?
NO! I HAVEN'T!
WHERE HAVE YOU BEEN TODAY?
NOWHERE.
I'VE BEEN TO THE BANK. DRAWN THE MONEY OUT. ALL OF IT.
WHAT DID YOU DO THAT FOR?
MAY WANT IT SOON.
I DON'T KNOW WHAT YOU MEAN.
YOU KNOW YOU CAN TRUST ME.
"OH, YES. I CAN TRUST YOU. IF I HADN'T TRUSTED YOU I WOULDN'T HAVE MARRIED YOU.
"I SHOULD LIKE TO KNOW WHO'S FRIGHTENED YOU. YOU AIN'T A SLAVE, NO ONE NEED BE A SLAVE IN THIS COUNTRY--AND DON'T MAKE YOURSELF ONE.
"THE BUSINESS ISN'T SO BAD --YOU'VE A COMFORTABLE HOME.
RING RING
"SHOP, ADOLPH. YOU GO."
"WHAT'S THE MATTER?"
"I FIND I'LL HAVE TO GO OUT THIS EVENING."
YOU KNEW MR. VERLOC BEFORE--DIDN'T YOU?
I HAVE HEARD OF HIM.

I SAY, ADOLF, HE AIN'T ONE OF THEM EMBASSY PEOPLE YOU HAVE BEEN BOTHERED WITH OF LATE?
WHO'S BEEN TALKING TO YOU OF THE EMBASSY PEOPLE?
YOU'VE BEEN TALKING IN YOUR SLEEP--IT SEEMED MOSTLY NONSENSE.
"NONSENSE, EH! THE EMBASSY PEOPLE! I WOULD CUT THEIR HEARTS OUT ONE AFTER ANOTHER, BUT LET THEM LOOK OUT. I'VE GOT A TONGUE IN MY HEAD."
"WELL, GET RID OF THE MAN, WHOEVER HE IS, AS SOON AS YOU CAN, AND COME BACK HOME TO ME."
"ADOLF! WAIT! WHAT ABOUT THAT MONEY YOU DREW OUT? YOU'VE GOT IT IN YOUR POCKET? HADN'T YOU BETTER--"
Mrs. Verloc received it without another word.
This abode of her married life appeared to her as lonely and unsafe as though it had been situated in the midst of a forest.
RING RING
HUSBAND AT HOME, MRS. VERLOC?
NO, HE'S GONE OUT.
DASH ME IF I DIDN'T THINK SO! HE HASN'T LOST ANY TIME!
HE DIDN'T GO OUT ALONE --A STRANGER WHO CALLED.
WHAT IS GOING ON?
"THERE CAME INTO OUR HANDS -- WHAT WE BELIEVE IS--- A STOLEN OVERCOAT."
"WE HAVE LOST NO OVERCOAT."
"THAT'S FUNNY-- I SEE YOU KEEP A LOT OF MARKING INK HERE. THE OVER-COAT HAS A LABEL SEWN ON THE INSIDE WITH YOUR ADDRESS WRITTEN IN MARK-ING INK."
"THAT'S MY BROTHER'S, THEN."
"WHERE'S YOUR BROTHER? CAN I SEE HIM?"
HE'S BEEN AWAY LIVING WITH-- A FRIEND --IN THE COUNTRY.
"WHAT'S THE NAME OF THE FRIEND?"
MICHAELIS.
"JUST SO. CAPITAL. AND YOUR BROTHER NOW, WHAT'S HE LIKE--A STURDY, DARKISH CHAP--EH?"

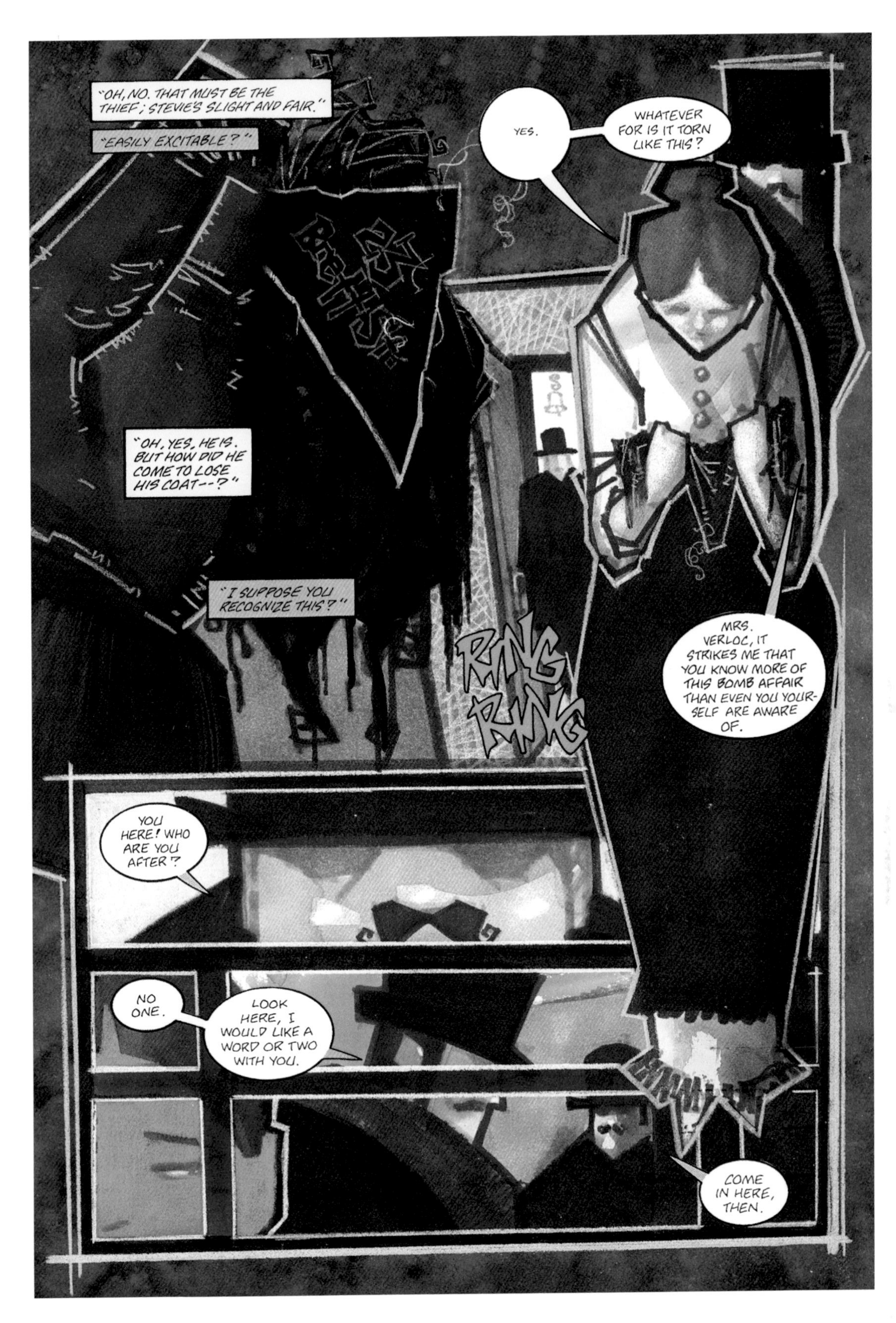
"OH, NO. THAT MUST BE THE THIEF; STEVIE'S SLIGHT AND FAIR."
"EASILY EXCITABLE?"
YES.
WHATEVER FOR IS IT TORN LIKE THIS?
"OH, YES, HE IS. BUT HOW DID HE COME TO LOSE HIS COAT--?"
"I SUPPOSE YOU RECOGNIZE THIS?"
MRS. VERLOC, IT STRIKES ME THAT YOU KNOW MORE OF THIS BOMB AFFAIR THAN EVEN YOU YOURSELF ARE AWARE OF.
RING RING
YOU HERE! WHO ARE YOU AFTER?
NO ONE.
LOOK HERE, I WOULD LIKE A WORD OR TWO WITH YOU.
COME IN HERE, THEN.

YOU ARE THE OTHER MAN, VERLOC. TWO MEN WERE SEEN ENTERING THE PARK.
WELL, TAKE ME NOW. WHAT'S TO PREVENT YOU? YOU HAVE THE RIGHT.
"OH NO! I KNOW TOO WELL WHO YOU HAVE BEEN GIVING YOURSELF AWAY TO. HE'LL HAVE TO MANAGE THIS LITTLE AFFAIR ALL BY HIMSELF. BUT DON'T YOU MAKE A MISTAKE. IT'S I WHO FOUND YOU."
"YOU MUST HAVE BEEN MAD."
"I HAVE BEEN MAD FOR A MONTH OR MORE, BUT I AM NOT MAD NOW. IT'S ALL OVER. IT SHALL COME OUT, AND HANG THE CONSEQUENCES."
"DON'T YOU TRUST SO MUCH TO WHAT YOU HAVE BEEN PROMISED. IF I WERE YOU I WOULD CLEAR OUT. I DON'T THINK WE WILL RUN AFTER YOU."
"OH, YES; YOU HOPE THE OTHERS WILL GET RID OF ME FOR YOU--DON'T YOU? NO, NO, I HAVE BEEN A STRAIGHT MAN TO THOSE PEOPLE TOO LONG, AND NOW EVERYTHING MUST COME OUT."
"LET IT COME OUT, THEN. BUT TELL ME NOW: HOW DID YOU GET AWAY?"
"I WAS MAKING FOR CHESTERFIELD WALK WHEN I HEARD THE BANG. I STARTED RUNNING THEN. FOG. I SAW NO ONE TILL I WAS PAST THE END OF GEORGE STREET."
"SO EASY AS THAT! THE BANG STARTLED YOU, EH?"
"YES, IT CAME TOO SOON."
"WE BELIEVE HE STUMBLED AGAINST THE ROOT OF A TREE."

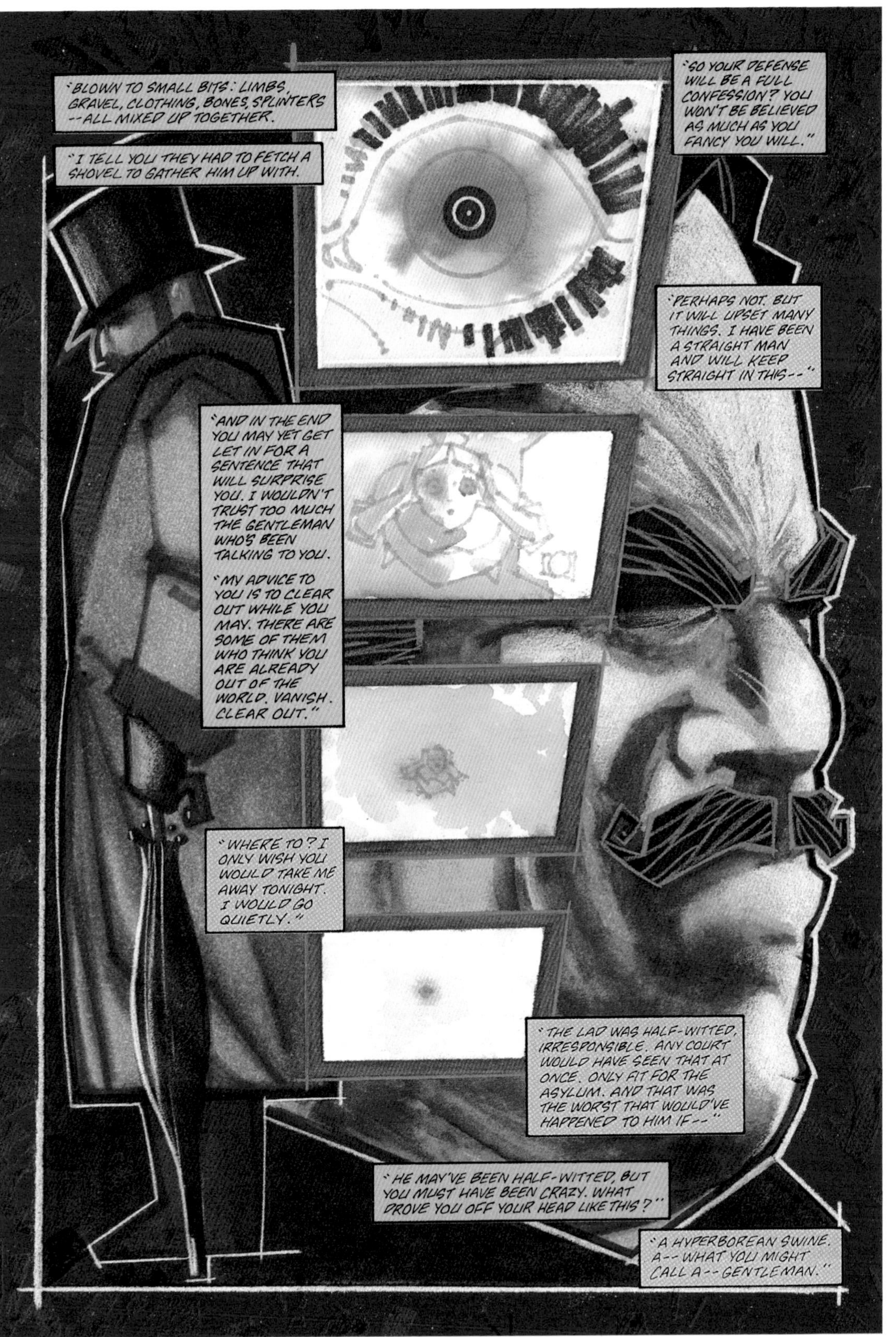
"BLOWN TO SMALL BITS: LIMBS, GRAVEL, CLOTHING, BONES, SPLINTERS --ALL MIXED UP TOGETHER.
"I TELL YOU THEY HAD TO FETCH A SHOVEL TO GATHER HIM UP WITH.
"SO YOUR DEFENSE WILL BE A FULL CONFESSION? YOU WON'T BE BELIEVED AS MUCH AS YOU FANCY YOU WILL."
"PERHAPS NOT. BUT IT WILL UPSET MANY THINGS. I HAVE BEEN A STRAIGHT MAN AND WILL KEEP STRAIGHT IN THIS--"
"AND IN THE END YOU MAY YET GET LET IN FOR A SENTENCE THAT WILL SURPRISE YOU. I WOULDN'T TRUST TOO MUCH THE GENTLEMAN WHO'S BEEN TALKING TO YOU.
"MY ADVICE TO YOU IS TO CLEAR OUT WHILE YOU MAY. THERE ARE SOME OF THEM WHO THINK YOU ARE ALREADY OUT OF THE WORLD. VANISH. CLEAR OUT."
"WHERE TO? I ONLY WISH YOU WOULD TAKE ME AWAY TONIGHT. I WOULD GO QUIETLY."
"THE LAD WAS HALF-WITTED, IRRESPONSIBLE. ANY COURT WOULD HAVE SEEN THAT AT ONCE. ONLY FIT FOR THE ASYLUM. AND THAT WAS THE WORST THAT WOULD'VE HAPPENED TO HIM IF--"
"HE MAY'VE BEEN HALF-WITTED, BUT YOU MUST HAVE BEEN CRAZY. WHAT DROVE YOU OFF YOUR HEAD LIKE THIS?"
"A HYPERBOREAN SWINE. A--WHAT YOU MIGHT CALL A--GENTLEMAN."

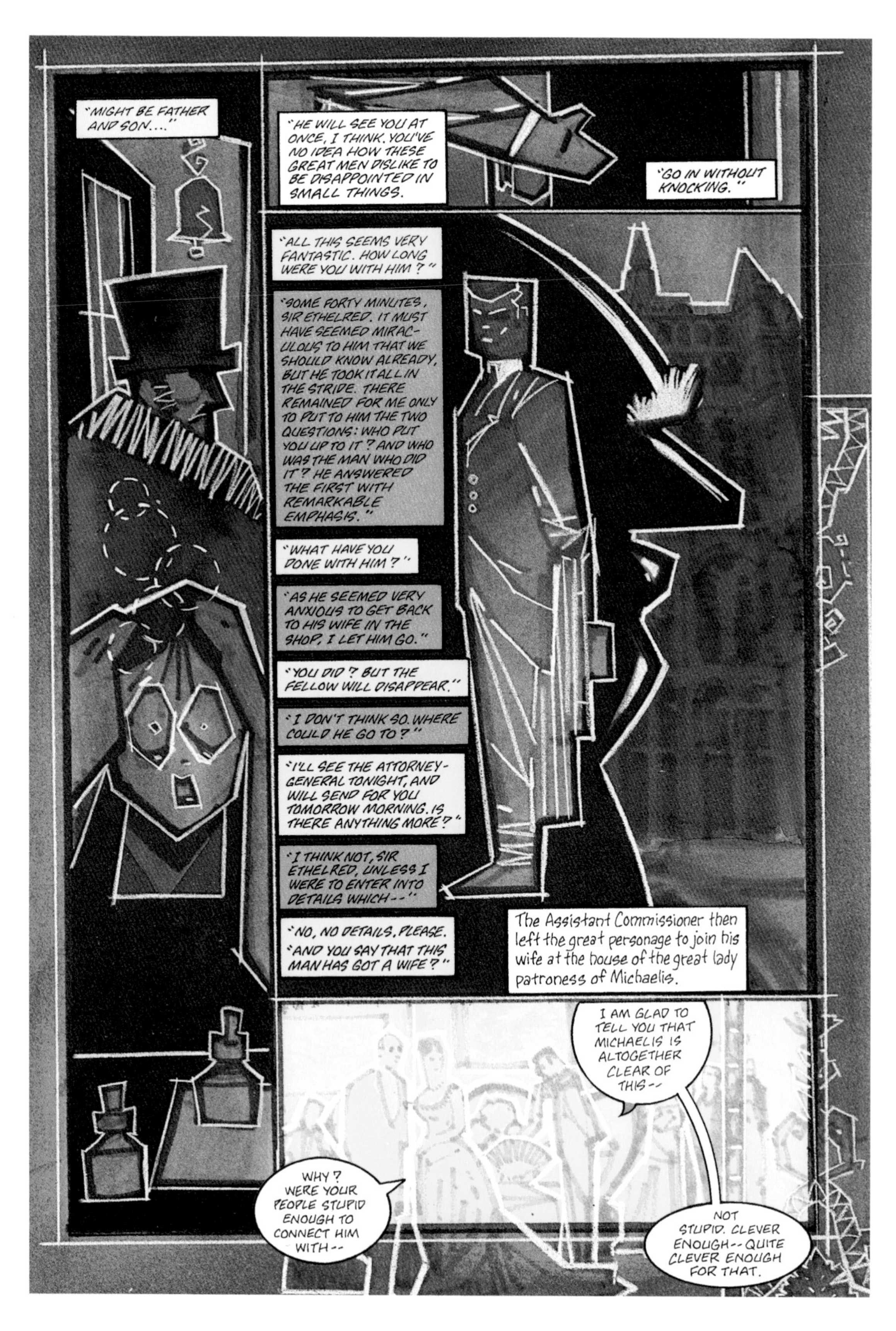
"MIGHT BE FATHER AND SON..."
"HE WILL SEE YOU AT ONCE, I THINK. YOU'VE NO IDEA HOW THESE GREAT MEN DISLIKE TO BE DISAPPOINTED IN SMALL THINGS.
"GO IN WITHOUT KNOCKING."
"ALL THIS SEEMS VERY FANTASTIC. HOW LONG WERE YOU WITH HIM?"
"SOME FORTY MINUTES, SIR ETHELRED. IT MUST HAVE SEEMED MIRACULOUS TO HIM THAT WE SHOULD KNOW ALREADY, BUT HE TOOK IT ALL IN THE STRIDE. THERE REMAINED FOR ME ONLY TO PUT TO HIM THE TWO QUESTIONS: WHO PUT YOU UP TO IT? AND WHO WAS THE MAN WHO DID IT? HE ANSWERED THE FIRST WITH REMARKABLE EMPHASIS."
"WHAT HAVE YOU DONE WITH HIM?"
"AS HE SEEMED VERY ANXIOUS TO GET BACK TO HIS WIFE IN THE SHOP, I LET HIM GO."
"YOU DID? BUT THE FELLOW WILL DISAPPEAR."
"I DON'T THINK SO. WHERE COULD HE GO TO?"
"I'LL SEE THE ATTORNEY-GENERAL TONIGHT, AND WILL SEND FOR YOU TOMORROW MORNING. IS THERE ANYTHING MORE?"
"I THINK NOT, SIR ETHELRED, UNLESS I WERE TO ENTER INTO DETAILS WHICH--"
"NO, NO DETAILS, PLEASE.
"AND YOU SAY THAT THIS MAN HAS GOT A WIFE?"
The Assistant Commissioner then left the great personage to join his wife at the house of the great lady patroness of Michaelis.
I AM GLAD TO TELL YOU THAT MICHAELIS IS ALTOGETHER CLEAR OF THIS--
WHY? WERE YOUR PEOPLE STUPID ENOUGH TO CONNECT HIM WITH--
NOT STUPID. CLEVER ENOUGH--QUITE CLEVER ENOUGH FOR THAT.

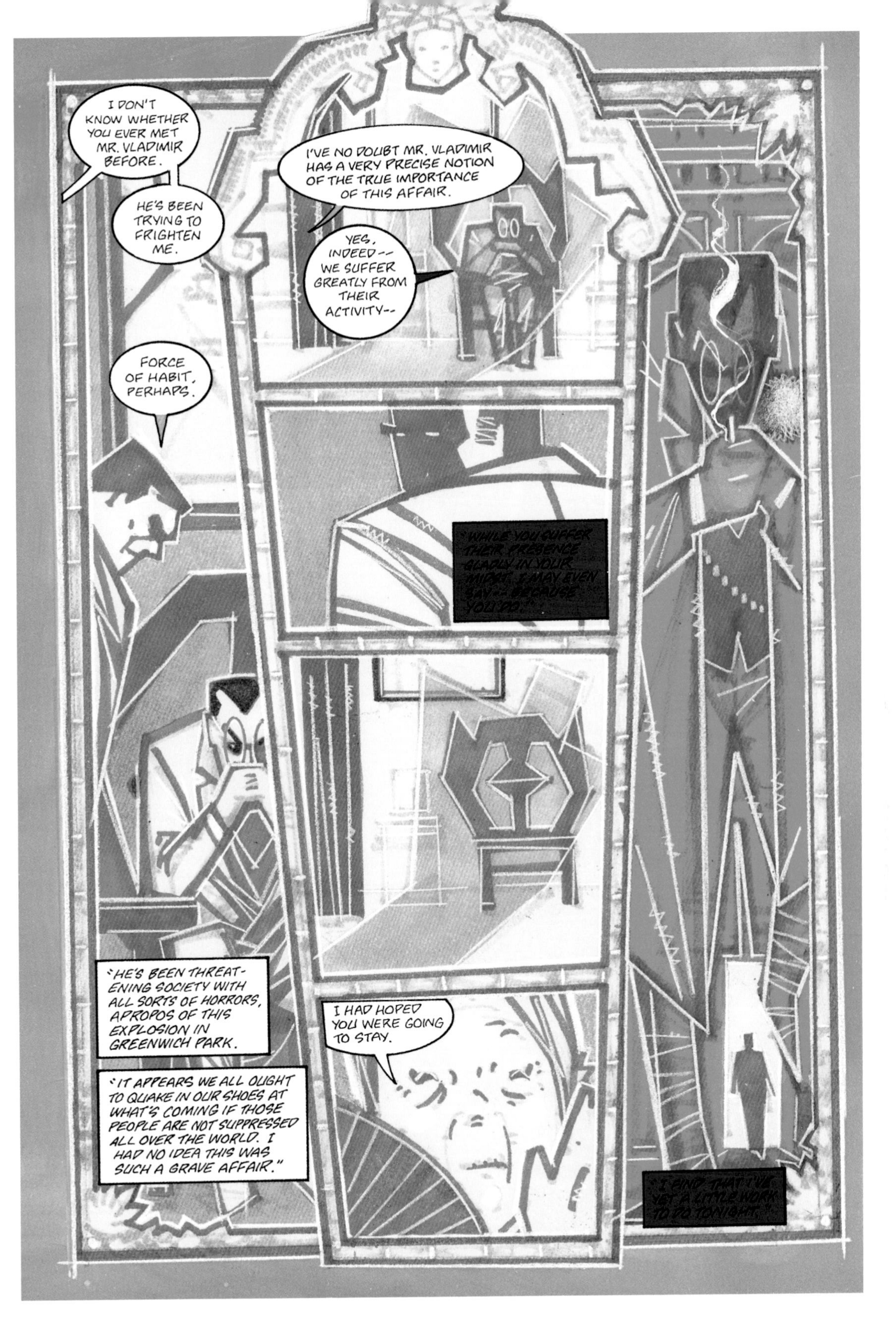

I DON'T KNOW WHETHER YOU EVER MET MR. VLADIMIR BEFORE.
HE'S BEEN TRYING TO FRIGHTEN ME.
I'VE NO DOUBT MR. VLADIMIR HAS A VERY PRECISE NOTION OF THE TRUE IMPORTANCE OF THIS AFFAIR.
YES, INDEED-- WE SUFFER GREATLY FROM THEIR ACTIVITY--
FORCE OF HABIT, PERHAPS.
"WHILE YOU SUFFER THEIR PRESENCE GLADLY IN YOUR MIDST, I MAY EVEN SAY--BECAUSE YOU DO."
"HE'S BEEN THREAT-ENING SOCIETY WITH ALL SORTS OF HORRORS, APROPOS OF THIS EXPLOSION IN GREENWICH PARK.
"IT APPEARS WE ALL OUGHT TO QUAKE IN OUR SHOES AT WHAT'S COMING IF THOSE PEOPLE ARE NOT SUPPRESSED ALL OVER THE WORLD. I HAD NO IDEA THIS WAS SUCH A GRAVE AFFAIR."
I HAD HOPED YOU WERE GOING TO STAY.
"I FIND THAT I'VE YET A LITTLE WORK TO DO TONIGHT."

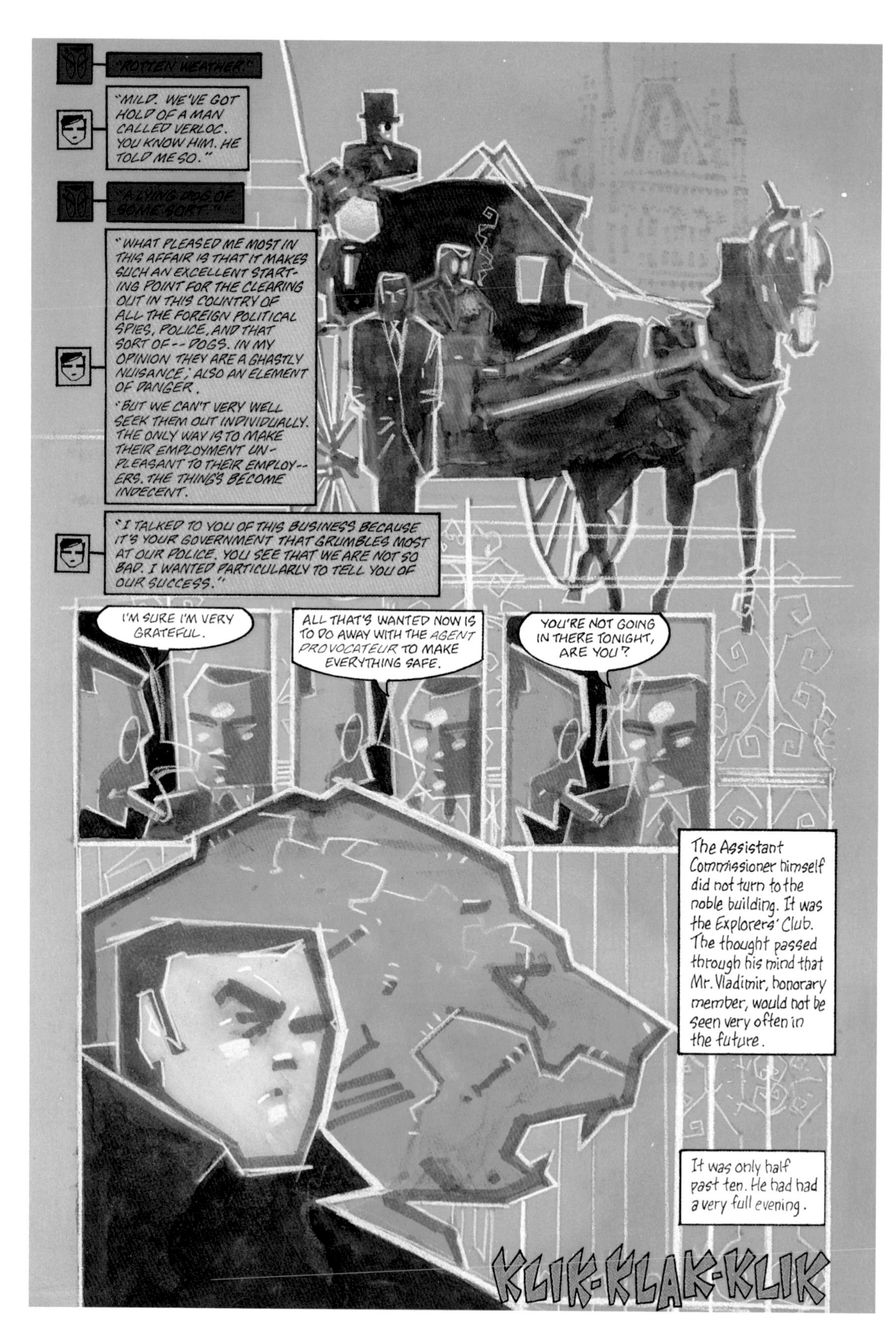

"ROTTEN WEATHER."
"MILD. WE'VE GOT HOLD OF A MAN CALLED VERLOC. YOU KNOW HIM. HE TOLD ME SO."
"A LYING DOG OF SOME SORT."
"WHAT PLEASED ME MOST IN THIS AFFAIR IS THAT IT MAKES SUCH AN EXCELLENT STARTING POINT FOR THE CLEARING OUT IN THIS COUNTRY OF ALL THE FOREIGN POLITICAL SPIES, POLICE, AND THAT SORT OF -- DOGS. IN MY OPINION THEY ARE A GHASTLY NUISANCE; ALSO AN ELEMENT OF DANGER.
"BUT WE CAN'T VERY WELL SEEK THEM OUT INDIVIDUALLY. THE ONLY WAY IS TO MAKE THEIR EMPLOYMENT UNPLEASANT TO THEIR EMPLOYERS. THE THING'S BECOME INDECENT.
"I TALKED TO YOU OF THIS BUSINESS BECAUSE IT'S YOUR GOVERNMENT THAT GRUMBLES MOST AT OUR POLICE. YOU SEE THAT WE ARE NOT SO BAD. I WANTED PARTICULARLY TO TELL YOU OF OUR SUCCESS."
I'M SURE I'M VERY GRATEFUL.
ALL THAT'S WANTED NOW IS TO DO AWAY WITH THE AGENT PROVOCATEUR TO MAKE EVERYTHING SAFE.
YOU'RE NOT GOING IN THERE TONIGHT, ARE YOU?
The Assistant Commissioner himself did not turn to the noble building. It was the Explorers' Club. The thought passed through his mind that Mr. Vladimir, honorary member, would not be seen very often in the future.
It was only half past ten. He had had a very full evening.
KLIK-KLAK-KLIK

TIK TIK TIK TIK TIK TIK TIK TIK
"I DIDN'T MEAN ANY HARM TO THE BOY.
"DO BE REASONABLE. YOU DON'T KNOW WHAT A BRUTE I HAD TO DEAL WITH. A MAN LIKE ME! LOOK HERE! SOME OF THE HIGHEST IN THE WORLD GOT TO THANK ME FOR WALKING ON THEIR TWO LEGS TO THIS DAY. THAT'S THE MAN YOU'VE GOT MARRIED TO, MY GIRL!
"THERE ISN'T A MURDERING PLOT FOR THE LAST ELEVEN YEARS THAT I HADN'T MY FINGER IN AT THE RISK OF MY LIFE. THERE'S SCORES OF THESE REVOLUTIONISTS I'VE SENT OFF WITH THEIR BOMBS IN THEIR BLAMED POCKETS, TO GET THEMSELVES CAUGHT ON THE FRONTIER. THE OLD BARON KNEW WHAT I WAS WORTH TO HIS COUNTRY. AND HERE SUDDENLY A SWINE COMES ALONG-- AN IGNORANT, OVERBEARING SWINE."
"CAN'T BE HELPED. COME, WINNIE, WE'VE GOT TO THINK OF TOMORROW. YOU'LL WANT ALL YOUR WITS ABOUT YOU AFTER I AM TAKEN AWAY."
"YOU TOOK THE BOY AWAY TO MURDER HIM."
"I WISH TO GOODNESS I HAD NEVER SEEN GREENWICH PARK OR ANYTHING BELONGING TO IT."
MIGHT HAVE BEEN FATHER AND SON.
"YOU TOOK THE BOY AWAY..."
"WINNIE."
YES.
COME HERE.

SHE KNOWS ALL ABOUT IT NOW.
"YOU MIGHT LOOK AT A FELLOW."
I DON'T WANT TO LOOK AT YOU AS LONG AS I LIVE.
I DIDN'T MEAN ANY HARM TO COME TO THE BOY.
KTIK TIK TIK TIK TIK TIK TIK TIK
"IT'S THAT DAMNED HEAT. HE'S UPSET YOU. HE'S A BRUTE, BLURTING IT OUT LIKE THAT TO A WOMAN."
"I DIDN'T FEEL PARTICULARLY GAY SITTING THERE AND THINKING OF YOU.
"DO BE REASONABLE, WINNIE. WHAT WOULD IT HAVE BEEN IF YOU HAD LOST ME?"

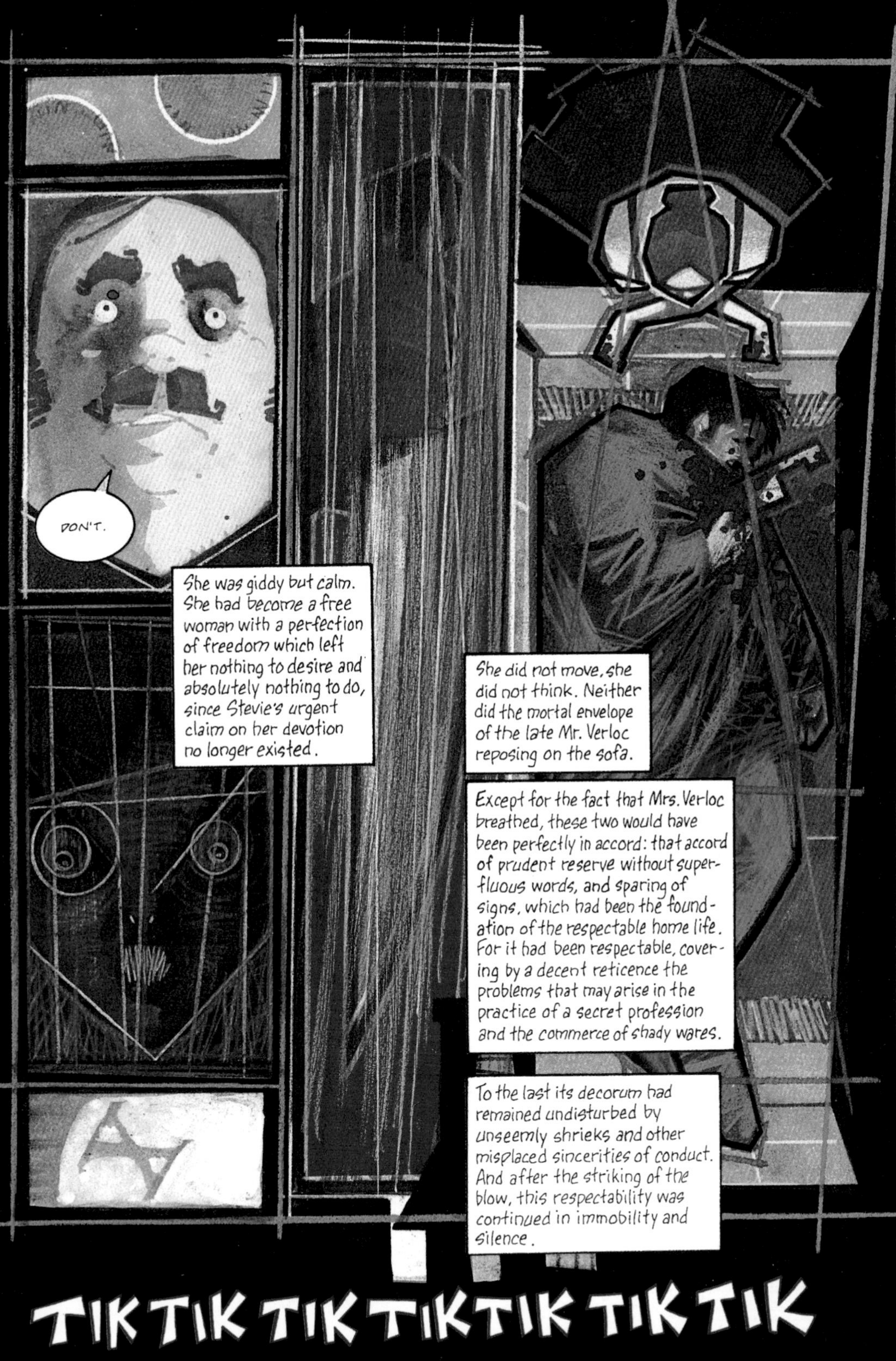
DON'T.
She was giddy but calm. She had become a free woman with a perfection of freedom which left her nothing to desire and absolutely nothing to do, since Stevie's urgent claim on her devotion no longer existed.
She did not move, she did not think. Neither did the mortal envelope of the late Mr. Verloc reposing on the sofa.
Except for the fact that Mrs. Verloc breathed, these two would have been perfectly in accord: that accord of prudent reserve without superfluous words, and sparing of signs, which had been the foundation of the respectable home life. For it had been respectable, covering by a decent reticence the problems that may arise in the practice of a secret profession and the commerce of shady wares.
To the last its decorum had remained undisturbed by unseemly shrieks and other misplaced sincerities of conduct. And after the striking of the blow, this respectability was continued in immobility and silence.
TIK TIK TIK TIKTIK TIK TIK

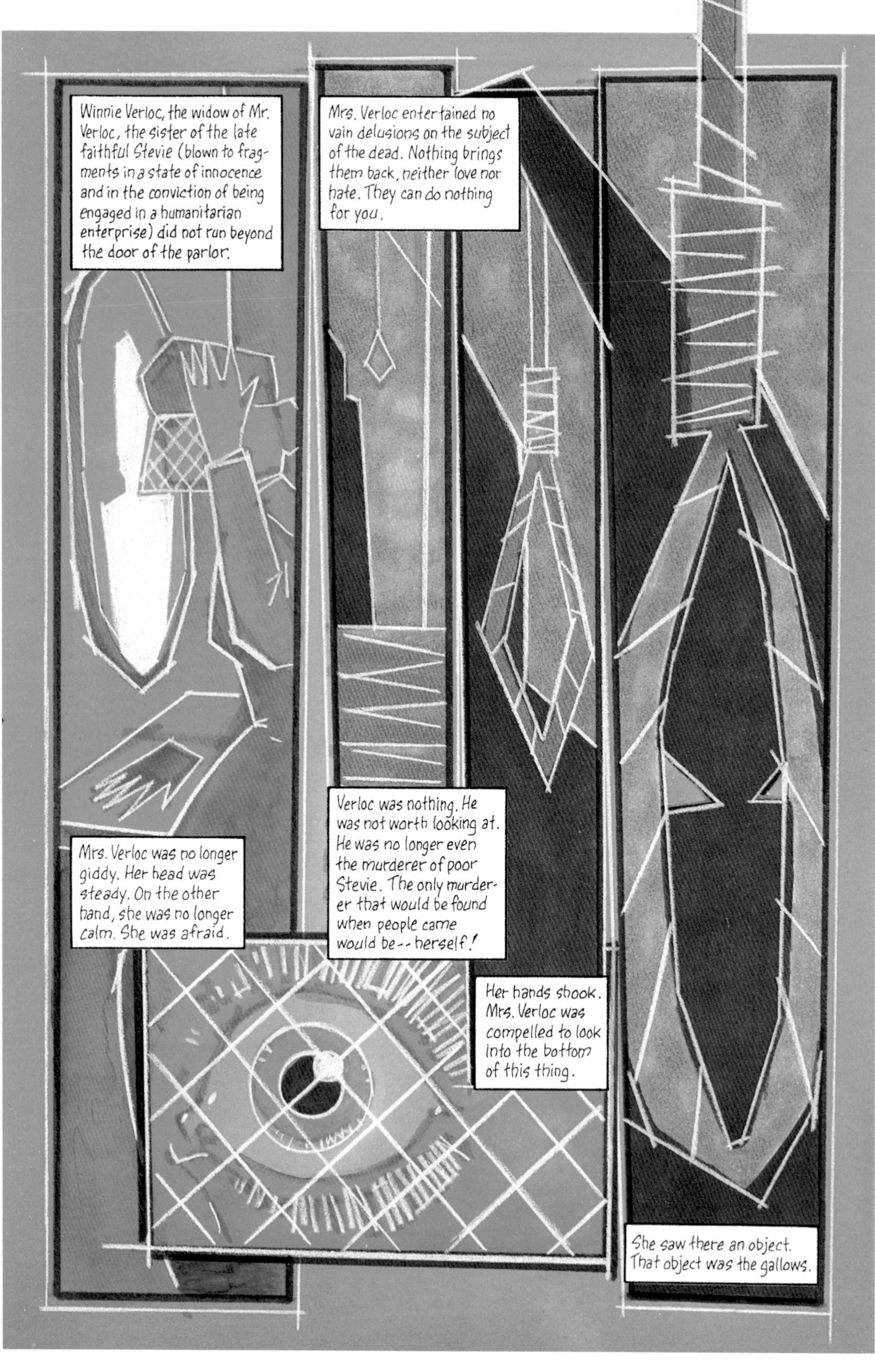
Winnie Verloc, the widow of Mr. Verloc, the sister of the late faithful Stevie (blown to fragments in a state of innocence and in the conviction of being engaged in a humanitarian enterprise) did not run beyond the door of the parlor.
Mrs. Verloc entertained no vain delusions on the subject of the dead. Nothing brings them back, neither love nor hate. They can do nothing for you.
Mrs. Verloc was no longer giddy. Her head was steady. On the other hand, she was no longer calm. She was afraid.
Verloc was nothing. He was not worth looking at. He was no longer even the murderer of poor Stevie. The only murderer that would be found when people came would be--herself!
Her hands shook. Mrs. Verloc was compelled to look into the bottom of this thing.
She saw there an object. That object was the gallows.

The street frightened her, since it led either to the gallows or to the river. She had no acquaintances of her own. Nobody would miss her in a social way. Winnie had been a good daughter because she had been a devoted sister. Her mother had always leaned on her for support. Now that Stevie was dead the bonds seemed to be broken. She could not face the old woman with the horrible tale. Moreover, it was too far. The river was her present destination. Mrs. Verloc tried to forget her mother.
MR. OSSIPON!
MRS. VERLOC? YOU HERE!
"YOU RECOGNIZED ME."
OF COURSE I DID. I'VE THOUGHT OF YOU TOO OFTEN LATELY NOT TO RECOGNIZE YOU ANYWHERE, AT ANY TIME. I'VE ALWAYS THOUGHT OF YOU--EVER SINCE I FIRST SET EYES ON YOU.
YES.
"I THOUGHT SO."
YOU'VE READ IT IN MY EYES.
"A LOVE LIKE MINE COULD NOT BE CONCEALED FROM A WOMAN LIKE YOU. I DARE SAY YOU COULD NOT HELP SEEING IT IN MY EYES. BUT I COULD NOT GUESS IT. YOU WERE ALWAYS SO DISTANT--"
"WHAT ELSE DID YOU EXPECT? I WAS A RESPECTABLE WOMAN--"
"HE NEVER DID SEEM TO ME TO BE QUITE WORTHY OF YOU. YOU WERE WORTHY OF A BETTER FATE."
"BETTER FATE! HE CHEATED ME OUT OF SEVEN YEARS OF LIFE. SEVEN YEARS A GOOD WIFE TO HIM, THE KIND, THE GOOD, THE GENEROUS, THE --AND HE LOVED ME. OH, YES, HE LOVED ME 'TILL I SOMETIMES WISHED MYSELF--SEVEN YEARS, SEVEN YEARS A WIFE TO HIM. AND DO YOU KNOW WHAT HE WAS, THAT DEAR FRIEND OF YOURS? DO YOU KNOW WHAT HE WAS?--HE WAS A DEVIL!"
"NO, I DIDN'T KNOW. BUT I DO KNOW NOW. I--UNDERSTAND. UNHAPPY, BRAVE WOMAN!"
"YOU MUST HIDE ME 'TILL THE MORNING SOMEWHERE."
"IT WOULD BE POSSIBLE PERHAPS TO FIND SAFE LODGING SOMEWHERE, BUT THE TRUTH IS, MY DEAR, I HAVE NOT ENOUGH MONEY TO GO AND TRY WITH--ONLY A FEW PENCE. WE REVOLUTIONISTS ARE NOT RICH. AND THERE'S THE JOURNEY BEFORE US TOO --FIRST THING IN THE MORNING AT THAT."
"BUT I HAVE--I HAVE MONEY. I HAVE ENOUGH MONEY. LET US GO FROM HERE."
"HOW MUCH HAVE YOU GOT?"
"I HAVE MONEY, I TELL YOU. ALL THE MONEY."
"WHAT DO YOU MEAN BY IT? ALL THE MONEY THERE WAS IN THE BANK, OR WHAT?"
"YES, YES! ALL THERE WAS. HE GAVE IT TO ME."
"WHY, THEN--WE ARE SAVED."

"YOU WILL SAVE ME! HIDE ME. DON'T LET THEM HAVE ME. YOU MUST KILL ME FIRST. I COULDN'T DO IT MYSELF-- I COULDN'T, I COULDN'T--NOT EVEN FOR WHAT I AM AFRAID OF."
"WHAT THE DEVIL ARE YOU AFRAID OF?"
"HAVEN'T YOU GUESSED WHAT I WAS DRIVEN TO DO?
"I WILL NOT BE HANGED! I WILL NOT--"
"YOU DID THIS THING QUITE BY YOURSELF? I WOULDN'T HAVE BELIEVED IT POSSIBLE, NOBODY WOULD."
DON'T LET THEM HANG ME! TAKE ME OUT OF THE COUNTRY. I'LL WORK FOR YOU. I'LL SLAVE FOR YOU. I'LL LOVE YOU. I'VE NO ONE IN THE WORLD. WHO WOULD LOOK AT ME IF YOU DON'T? I WON'T ASK YOU TO MARRY ME.
WAS HE ASLEEP?
NO! HE WASN'T. HE HAD BEEN TELLING ME THAT NOTHING COULD TOUCH HIM. AFTER TAKING THE BOY AWAY FROM UNDER MY VERY EYES TO KILL HIM--THE LOVING, INNOCENT, HARMLESS LAD. MY OWN, I TELL YOU.
AND HE SAYS TO ME LIKE THIS: "COME HERE," AFTER TELLING ME SUCH THINGS--AFTER TAKING MY VERY HEART OUT OF ME ALONG WITH THE BOY TO SMASH IN THE DIRT.
BLOOD AND DIRT. BLOOD AND DIRT.
A great light broke upon Comrade Ossipon. It was that half-witted lad who had perished in the park. And the fooling of everybody all around appeared more complete than ever--colossal.
"THE DEGENERATE --BY HEAVENS!"
"WHAT DID HE THINK I WAS MADE OF? COME HERE! ME! LIKE THIS! OH, YES! I CAME--FOR THE LAST TIME-- WITH THE KNIFE."
"HELP! SAVE ME. I WON'T BE HANGED!"
"LET'S GET OUT, OR WE WILL LOSE THE TRAIN. WHERE ARE WE GOING TO? LET'S GET TO PARIS FIRST, THE BEST WAY WE CAN--GO OUT FIRST, AND SEE IF THE WAY IS CLEAR."
"IT'S ALL RIGHT."

"WHEN WE ARRIVE, YOU MUST GO INTO THE STATION AHEAD OF ME, AS IF WE DID NOT KNOW EACH OTHER. I WILL TAKE THE TICKETS, AND SLIP YOURS INTO YOUR HAND, AS I PASS YOU. THEN YOU WILL GO INTO THE FIRST-CLASS LADIES' WAITING-ROOM AND SIT THERE UNTIL TEN MINUTES BEFORE THE TRAIN STARTS. THEN YOU COME OUT. I WILL BE OUTSIDE. YOU GO IN FIRST ON THE PLATFORM AS IF YOU DID NOT KNOW ME. THERE MAY BE EYES WATCHING THERE THAT KNOW WHAT'S WHAT. DO YOU UNDERSTAND, MY DEAR?
"BY-THE-BY, I OUGHT TO HAVE THE MONEY FOR THE TICKETS NOW.
"DO YOU KNOW HOW MUCH MONEY IS IN THAT THING?"
"NO. HE GAVE IT TO ME. I DIDN'T COUNT. I THOUGHT NOTHING OF IT AT THE TIME."
"IN HERE, WINNIE."
"WHAT IS IT? IS THERE ANY DANGER?"
"WAIT A MOMENT. THERE'S THE GUARD."
I TOLD HIM NOT TO LET ANYONE INTO OUR COMPARTMENT.
YOU THINK OF EVERY-THING.
"THERE IS NO DANGER."
WOOWOO
"I WILL LIVE ALL OF MY DAYS FOR YOU!"
WOOWOO
CHUGGA CHUGGA
CHUGGA CHUGGA
CHUGGA CHUGGA
BONG BONG BONG BONG

"MICHAELIS DIDN'T KNOW ANYTHING OF VERLOC'S DEATH. OF COURSE! HE NEVER LOOKS AT THE NEWSPAPERS. THEY MAKE HIM TOO SAD, HE SAYS."
"COME AND DRINK SOME BEER WITH ME."
"BEER! SO BE IT! LET US DRINK AND BE MERRY, FOR WE ARE STRONG, AND TOMORROW, WE DIE."
WHAT'S THE MATTER, OSSIPON? YOU LOOK GLUM AND SEEK EVEN MY COMPANY. I HEAR THAT YOU ARE SEEN CONSTANTLY IN PLACES WHERE MEN UTTER FOOLISH THINGS OVER GLASSES OF LIQUOR. WHY? HAVE YOU ABANDONED YOUR COLLECTION OF WOMEN? THEY ARE THE WEAK WHO FEED THE STRONG, EH?
TELL ME, OSSIPON, HAS EVERY ONE OF YOUR VICTIMS KILLED HERSELF FOR YOU -- OR ARE YOUR TRIUMPHS SO FAR INCOMPLETE -- FOR BLOOD ALONE PUTS A SEAL ON GREATNESS? BLOOD. DEATH. LOOK AT HISTORY.
YOU BE DAMNED.
WHY? LET THAT BE THE HOPE OF THE WEAK, WHOSE THEOLOGY HAS INVENTED HELP FOR THE STRONG. OSSIPON, MY FEELING FOR YOU IS AMICABLE CONTEMPT. YOU COULDN'T KILL A FLY.
"WHAT'S THAT PAPER? ANYTHING IN IT?"
NOTHING. NOTHING WHATSOEVER. THE THING'S TEN DAYS OLD. I FORGOT IT IN MY POCKET, I SUPPOSE.
The stewardess then went on deck to look for her, and found the unhappy lady lying down in one of the hooded seats. Her eyes were open, but she would not answer anything that was said to her. She seemed very ill. The stewardess fetched the chief steward, and those two people stood by the side of the hooded seat consulting over their extraordinary and tragic passenger.
Comrade Ossipon was well informed. He knew what the gangway man and the stewardess of the steamer had seen: a lady in black with a white face standing in the middle of a cabin. The lady seemed unwilling to speak, and as if she were in some awful trouble. The next the stewardess knew she was gone from the cabin.
Then they went away to arrange for removal down below, for indeed by what they could see of her face she seemed to them to be dying.

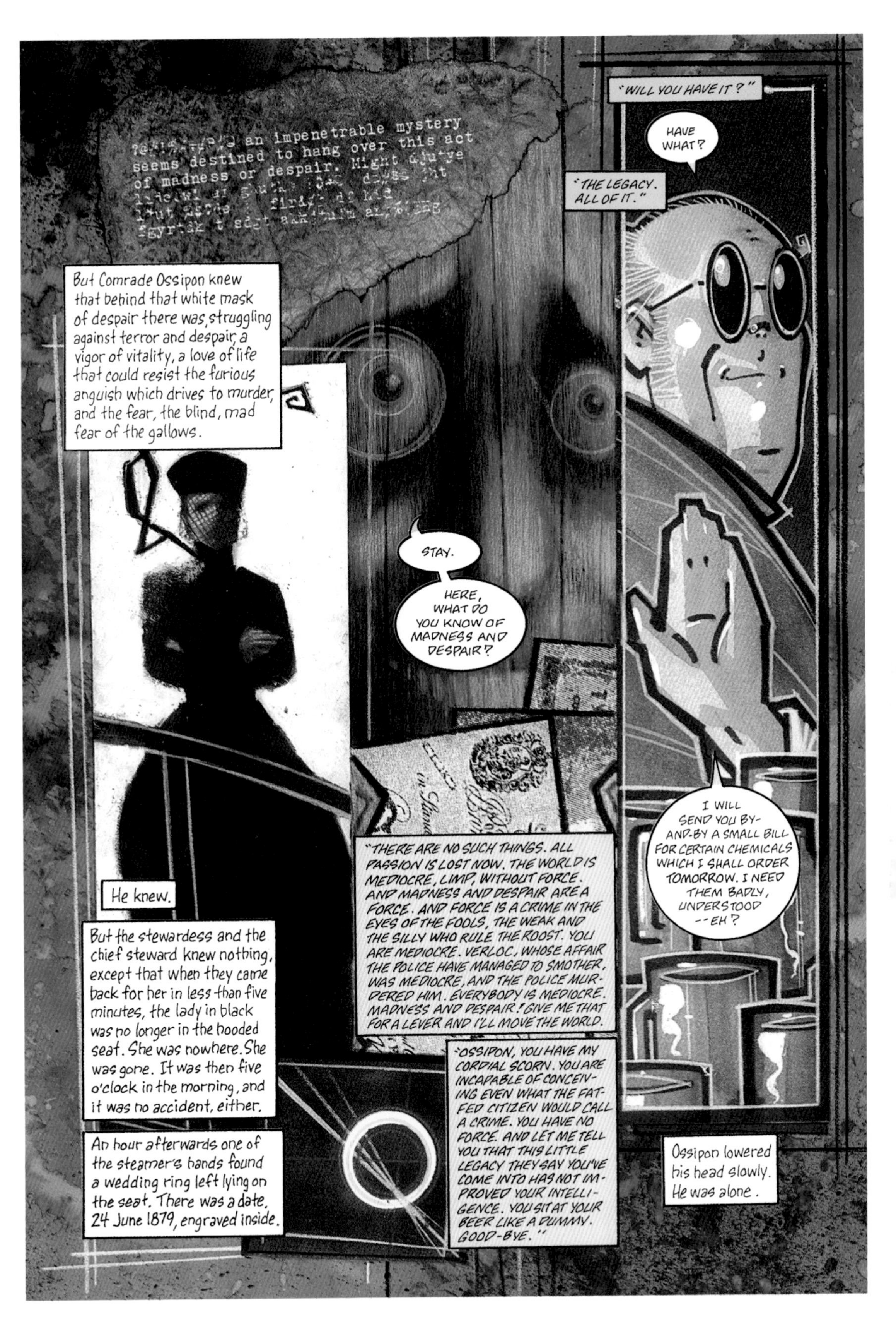
an impenetrable mystery seems destined to hang over this act of madness or despair.
But Comrade Ossipon knew that behind that white mask of despair there was, struggling against terror and despair, a vigor of vitality, a love of life that could resist the furious anguish which drives to murder, and the fear, the blind, mad fear of the gallows.
He knew.
But the stewardess and the chief steward knew nothing, except that when they came back for her in less than five minutes, the lady in black was no longer in the hooded seat. She was nowhere. She was gone. It was then five o'clock in the morning, and it was no accident, either.
An hour afterwards one of the steamer's hands found a wedding ring left lying on the seat. There was a date, 24 June 1879, engraved inside.
STAY.
HERE, WHAT DO YOU KNOW OF MADNESS AND DESPAIR?
"THERE ARE NO SUCH THINGS. ALL PASSION IS LOST NOW. THE WORLD IS MEDIOCRE, LIMP, WITHOUT FORCE. AND MADNESS AND DESPAIR ARE A FORCE. AND FORCE IS A CRIME IN THE EYES OF THE FOOLS, THE WEAK AND THE SILLY WHO RULE THE ROOST. YOU ARE MEDIOCRE. VERLOC, WHOSE AFFAIR THE POLICE HAVE MANAGED TO SMOTHER, WAS MEDIOCRE, AND THE POLICE MURDERED HIM. EVERYBODY IS MEDIOCRE. MADNESS AND DESPAIR! GIVE ME THAT FOR A LEVER AND I'LL MOVE THE WORLD.
"OSSIPON, YOU HAVE MY CORDIAL SCORN. YOU ARE INCAPABLE OF CONCEIVING EVEN WHAT THE FAT-FED CITIZEN WOULD CALL A CRIME. YOU HAVE NO FORCE. AND LET ME TELL YOU THAT THIS LITTLE LEGACY THEY SAY YOU'VE COME INTO HAS NOT IMPROVED YOUR INTELLIGENCE. YOU SIT AT YOUR BEER LIKE A DUMMY. GOOD-BYE."
"WILL YOU HAVE IT?"
HAVE WHAT?
"THE LEGACY. ALL OF IT."
I WILL SEND YOU BY-AND-BY A SMALL BILL FOR CERTAIN CHEMICALS WHICH I SHALL ORDER TOMORROW. I NEED THEM BADLY, UNDERSTOOD--EH?
Ossipon lowered his head slowly. He was alone.

He walked along the street without looking where he put his feet; and he walked in a direction which would not bring him to the place of appointment with another lady. He was walking away from it. He could face no woman.
It was ruin. He could neither think, work, sleep nor eat. But he was beginning to drink with pleasure, with anticipation, with hope. It was ruin.
His revolutionary career, sustained by the sentiment and trustfulness of many women, was menaced by an impenetrable mystery--the mystery of a human brain pulsating wrongfully to the rhythm of journalistic phrases.
"...WILL HANG FOREVER OVER THIS ACT..."--IT WAS INCLINING TOWARDS THE GUTTER--"...OF MADNESS OR DESPAIR."
"I AM SERIOUSLY ILL."
And the incorruptible professor walked, too, averting his eyes from the odious multitude of mankind. He had no future. He disdained it. He was a force. His thoughts caressed the images of ruin and destruction. He walked, frail, insignificant, shabby, miserable--and terrible in the simplicity of his ideas calling madness and despair to the regeneration of the world.
Nobody looked at him.
He passed on unsuspected and deadly, like a pest in the street full of men.
THE END

WATCH OUT FOR PAPERCUTZ™

Welcome, Agent, to the seventeenth, spy-filled CLASSICS ILLUSTRATED graphic novel—featuring an amazing adaptation of Joseph Conrad's "The Secret Agent" by John K. Snyder III . My name's Salicrup, *James Salicrup* (You may call me Jim!), and I'm the (Editor-in-) Chief of P.A.P.E.R.C.U.T.Z.*, the organization devoted to publishing great graphic novels for all ages!

While Mr. Verloc is certainly on a very serious mission, other Agents of P.A.P.E.R.C.U.T.Z. are having a lot more fun. Eight year-old Nancy Drew is busy solving the partial disappearance of a work of art in NANCY DREW AND THE CLUE CREW #2 "Secret Sand Sleuths." Garfield's about to expose a bogus spy in GARFIELD & Co #8 "Secret Agent X." Posing as dance students, Julie, Lucie, and Alia plan to foil Carla's chances at a dance competition in DANCE CLASS #5 "To Russia, With Love." And even our fruitiest spy is out to spoil the mad schemes of Grapefinger in ANNOYING ORANGE #1 "Secret Agent Orange"!

But before I give you your new mission, allow me to bring you up to speed on certain activities right here at P.A.P.E.R.C.U.T.Z. HQ! None other than erstwhile Associate Editor Michael Petranek, has been given a new assignment. He's now the Editor of CLASSICS ILLUSTRATED and several other top P.A.P.E.R.C.U.T.Z. titles! He's been awarded his official License to Thrill, and we're confident he'll be using it wisely in the performance of his duties.

Your mission, if you choose to accept it, is to investigate "The Murders in the Rue Morgue and Other Tales" by Edgar Allan Poe. You'll be ably assisted by Inspector C, Auguste Dupin. On the following pages, you'll get a very short briefing, but you'll need to track down the complete case files yourself in CLASSICS ILLUSTRATED DELUXE #10. Suspected whereabouts—at the bookseller nearest you.

CLASSICS ILLUSTRATED will be back with Aesop's Fables, coming October 2013.

This message will self-destruct in about two hundred years.

Thanks, Jim

*P.A.P.E.R.C.U.T.Z. – Producing Awesome Publications Encompassing Remarkable Characters Underscoring Today's Zeitgeist

CLASSICS ILLUSTRATED DELUXE

GRAPHIC NOVELS FROM PAPERCUTZ

#1 "The Wind In The Willows"

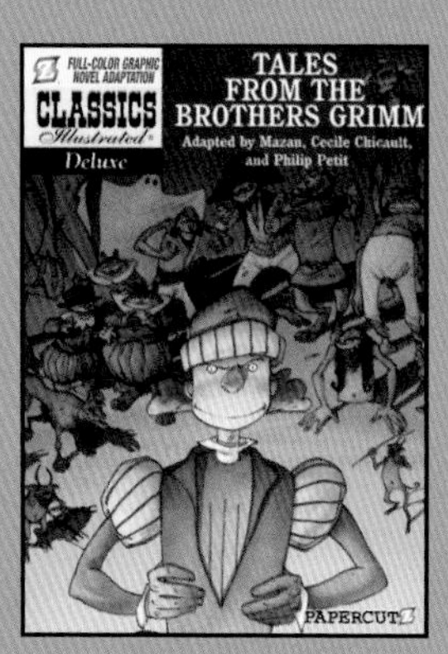

#2 "Tales From The Brothers Grimm"

#3 "Frankenstein"

#4 "The Adventures of Tom Sawyer"

#5 "Treasure Island"

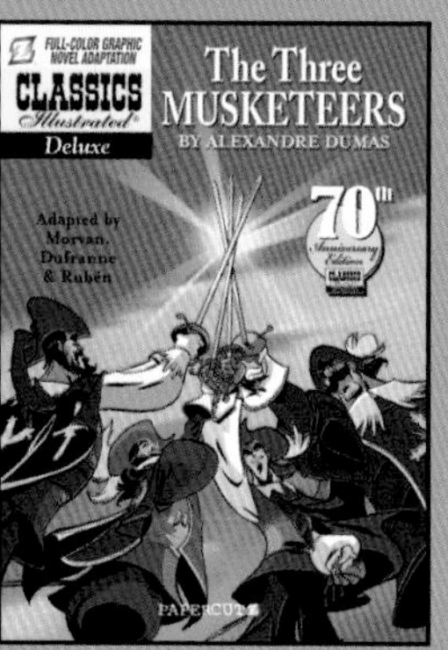

#6 "The Three Musketeers"

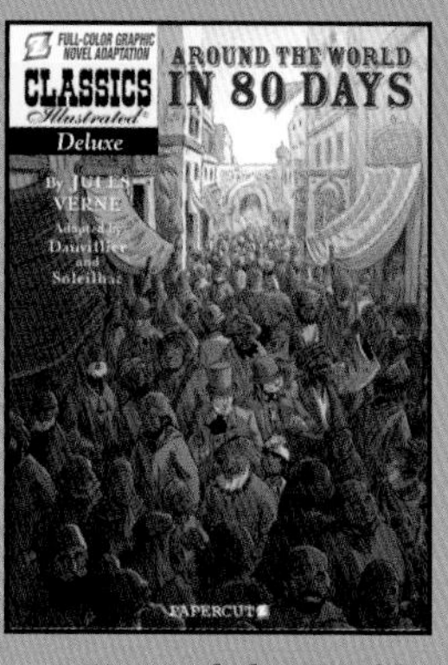

#7 "Around the World in 80 Days"

#8 "Oliver Twist"

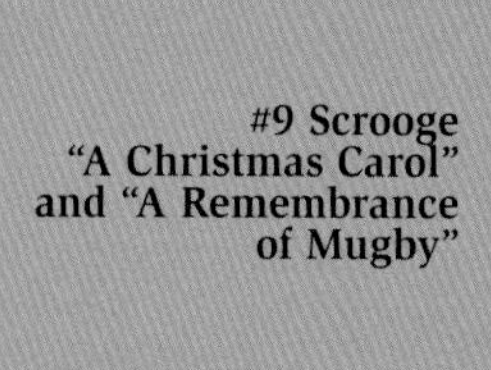

#9 Scrooge "A Christmas Carol" and "A Remembrance of Mugby"

Coming Soon: #10 "The Murders in the Rue Morgue and Other Tales"

CLASSICS ILLUSTRATED DELUXE graphic novels are available for $13.95 each in paperback and $17.95 in hardcover, except for #6, $16.99 pb., $21.99 hc, and #8, $19.99 pb., $24.99 hc. Please add $4.00 for postage and handling for the first book, add $1.00 for each additional book. MC, Visa, Amex accepted or make check payable to NBM Publishing. Send to: Papercutz, 160 Broadway, Suite 700, East Wing, New York, NY 10038 • 1-800-886-1223

OR ORDER FROM: WWW.PAPERCUTZ.COM

"WE'RE BACK!"
JACK LAKE
PRODUCTIONS INC.
CLASSICS Illustrated
THE THREE MUSKETEERS
THE LAST OF THE MOHICANS
MOBY DICK
A TALE OF TWO CITIES
GULLIVER'S TRAVELS
HUCKLEBERRY FINN
FRANKENSTEIN
SWISS FAMILY ROBINSON
20,000 LEAGUES UNDER THE SEA
BLACK BEAUTY
TREASURE ISLAND
THE CALL OF THE WILD
THE TIME MACHINE
ROMEO and JULIET
THE AENEID
A JOURNEY TO THE CENTER OF THE EARTH
The Story of AMERICA
THE WAR BETWEEN THE STATES
FREE
36" x 27"
POSTER
with purchase of 10 or more titles.

JOSEPH CONRAD & JOHN K. SNYDER III

Joseph Conrad was born in the Ukraine on December 3, 1857, to Polish aristocrats. His parents, proud patriots, were members of the resistance movement that rebelled against the Czarist Russians who then occupied Poland. When Conrad was four, his father was arrested, and the family was exiled to northern Russia. Three years later, Conrad's mother died. Eventually, the Czarist regime permitted Conrad and his father to return to Poland. The happy homecoming, however, was cut short when Conrad's father died, and the youth was sent to live with an uncle. At the age of 16, Conrad embarked upon a career as a sailor. He whiled away the long, lonely voyages by studying diligently. Conrad mastered English on his own, and became a naturalized British subject in 1886. He quickly moved up the maritime ranks until he passed his master's examination and was awarded with command of merchant ships sailing for Africa and the Orient. In 1895, at the age of 38, Conrad decided to dedicate himself to writing; he married, became the father of two sons, and settled near London. Although he spent the remainder of his life land-bound, Conrad's love of the seafaring life and its exotic ports-of-call formed the basis for many of his works. His first works – *Almayer's Folly* (1895) and *An Outcast of the Islands* (1896) evidenced Conrad's early struggles with both English and the narrative technique. His next work, however, *The Nigger of the "Narcissus"* (1897), displayed a unique and powerful mastery of storytelling. In rather rapid succession, Conrad published *Lord Jim* (1900), *Youth* (1902), *Heart of Darkness* (1903), *Typhoon* (1902), *Nostromo* (1904), *The Mirror of the Sea* (1906) and *The Secret Agent* (1907). He collaborated with Ford Madox Brown on two novels, *The Inheritors* (1901) and *Romance* (1903), before a quarrel ended the relationship. Conrad achieved renown among his peers, such as Stephen Crane and Henry James, but his work generally was poorly received by both critics and the reading public. Changing literary tastes led to a swell of interest in Conrad's works in the 1920s; when he died in 1925, he was established as a leading novelist. His appeal diminished again in the 1930s, but a critical reappraisal in the following decade led to a sustained consensus that Conrad was among the most masterful writers who ever lived.

John K. Snyder III was born in Indiana in 1961, and attended George Mason University. He has taught high school art classes, and was editor-in-chief of the Washington, D.C., artists' newspaper *The Duckburg Times*. Snyder's credits include *Grendel, Grimjack, Nexus, Fashion in Action,* and *Prowler*. Snyder adapted and illustrated Robert Louis Stevenson's Dr. Jekyll & Mr. Hyde for CLASSICS ILLUSTRATED #9.

Special Excerpt from CLASSICS ILLUSTRATED DELUXE #10 "The Murders in the Rue Morgue and Other Tales"
By Edgar Allan Poe, Adapted by Jean David Morvan and Fabrice Druet

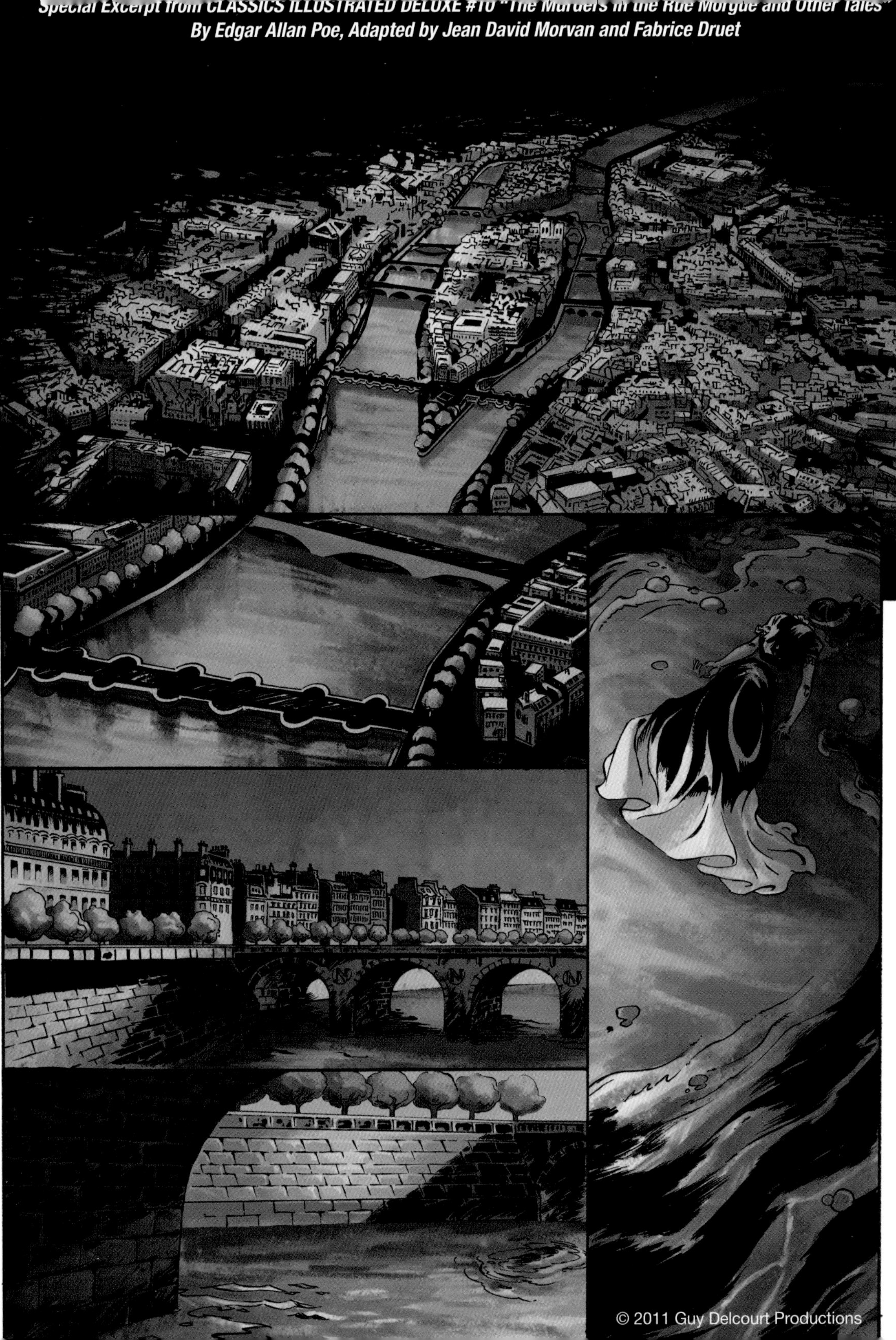

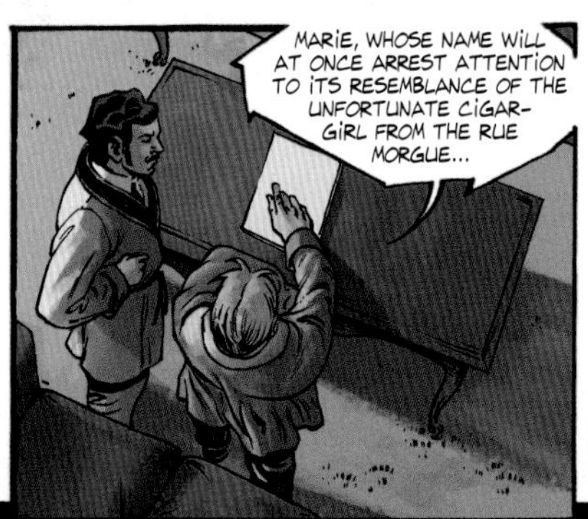
MARIE, WHOSE NAME WILL AT ONCE ARREST ATTENTION TO ITS RESEMBLANCE OF THE UNFORTUNATE CIGAR-GIRL FROM THE RUE MORGUE...

...WAS FOUND DROWNED IN THE SEINE.

THE DETAILS OF THE CRIME FOLLOW...

MARIE ROGET WAS THE ONLY DAUGHTER OF THE WIDOW ESTELLE ROGET. THE MOTHER AND DAUGHTER HAD DWELT TOGETHER IN THE RUE PAVEE...

...ON RUE SAINTANDRÉ

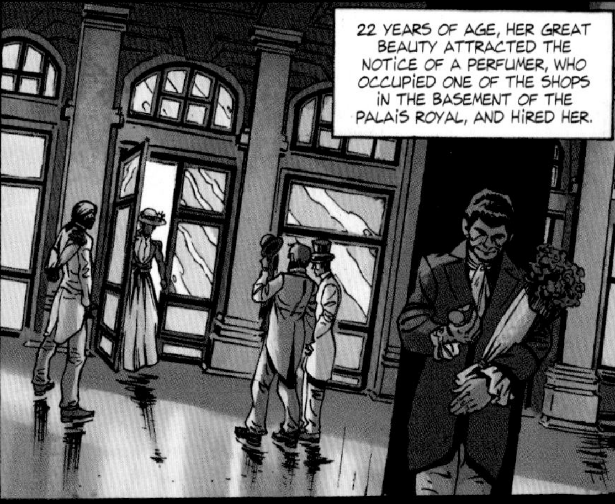
22 YEARS OF AGE, HER GREAT BEAUTY ATTRACTED THE NOTICE OF A PERFUMER, WHO OCCUPIED ONE OF THE SHOPS IN THE BASEMENT OF THE PALAIS ROYAL, AND HIRED HER.

THE ANTICIPATIONS OF THE SHOPKEEPER WERE REALIZED, AND HIS ROOMS SOON BECAME NOTORIOUS THROUGH THE CHARMS OF THE SPRIGHTLY GRISETTE.

SHE HAD BEEN IN HIS EMPLOY ABOUT A YEAR, WHEN HER ADMIRERS WERE THROWN INTO CONFUSION BY HER SUDDEN DISAPPEARANCE FROM THE SHOP.

MONSIEUR LE BLANC WAS UNABLE TO ACCOUNT FOR HER ABSENCE, AND MADAME ROGET WAS DISTRACTED WITH ANXIETY AND TERROR.

AFTER THE LAPSE OF A WEEK, MARIE, IN GOOD HEALTH, BUT WITH A SADDENED AIR, MADE HER REAPPEARANCE AT HER PERFUMERY.

THE GIRL, OSTENSIBLY TO RELIEVE HERSELF FROM THE IMPERTINENCE OF CURIOSITY, SOON BADE A FINAL ADIEU TO THE PERFUMER, AND SOUGHT THE SHELTER OF HER MOTHER'S RESIDENCE IN THE RUE PAVEE SAINT ANDREE.

IT WAS ABOUT FIVE MONTHS AFTER THIS RETURN HOME...

THAT HER FRIENDS WERE ALARMED BY HER SUDDEN DISAPPEARANCE FOR THE SECOND TIME.

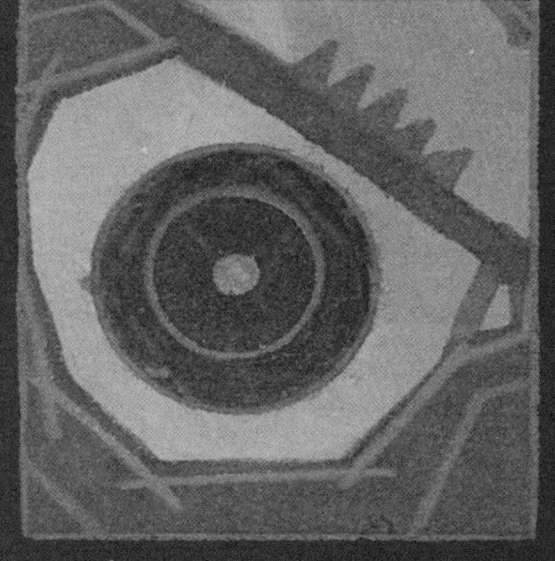
"I HAD TO TAKE THE CARVING KNIFE FROM THE BOY! HE CAN'T STAND THE NOTION OF ANY CRUELTY.

Oh. SHALL I PUT THE LIGHT OUT?

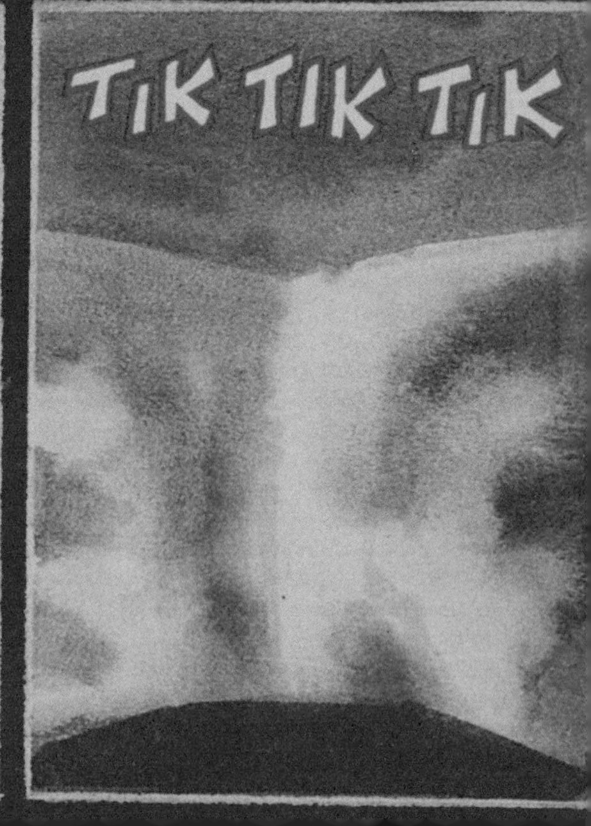
TIK TIK TIK